DANCE OF SHADOWS

CLINT WESTGARD

ALSO BY CLINT WESTGARD

The Shadow Men:

  Realm of Shadows

  Council of Shadows

  Dance of Shadows

The Sojourners Cycle:

  The Forgotten

  The Apostate

  The Acolyte (forthcoming)

  The Double (forthcoming)

  The Sojourner (forthcoming)

The Trials of the Minotaur

The Maleficio Chronicles

Published by Lost Quarter Books
www.lostquarterbooks.com

This edition 2015
Cover image : Deranged Doctor Designs
ISBN: 978-1-928035-07-7

For my family, for all their support.

CONTENTS

PRINCIPAL CHARACTERS

Craitol:

Lastl:

Donier a Fieled, noble of the third rank, officer in the Gver's army

Keleprai a Lastl, Gver of Lastl

Kigarle a Nepene, noble of the first rank in Lastl

Liene ul Terainous a Fusel, noble of rank in Lastl

Ludenn a Ghuerl, noble of rank, officer in the Gver's army

Niriese ul Keleprai a Vellar, wife of the Gver of Lastl

Craitol:

Alieren, Qraulla of the Realm

Dalenna ul Lestulatera, mother to the Qraul

Elihaun, Master of Offices for the Qraul

Laterala, Qraul of the Realm

Other Great Families:

Byuvir a Kylep, Gver of Kylep

Duirhe a Takyl, Gver of Takyl

Pervelte a Pysel, Gver of Pysel

Adepts:

Cepedutherupt, High Adept of the Council of Adepts

Hieran, disciple to Adept Tehh

Kercubegahedd, false Adept and leader of the Kragian rebellion

Tehh, Adept of Lastl

Vyissan, a Kragian and an Adept

Renuih:

Ad Eselte, emperor of Renuih

Ad Ezern:

Ctuellan, eunuch

Ibrazol id Ezern, Imperial Vazeir

Masiph den Ibrazol id Ezern, Jetthir of the Watch, son of Ibrazol

Ad Reteln:

Nyzrella (Nyzren) id Reteln, daughter of Osiphan

Osiphan id Reteln, nohritai in Darrhyn

Quesin, eunuch

Tequihan, castulan of the Ad Reteln household

Usyre id Reteln ys Luzyren, wife of Osiphan

Nohritai:

Erise id Illied, wife of Nustef

Gheyuth id Lelletl, Vazeir of the Renian Army

Nustef id Illied, second to Masiph on the Watch, husband of Erise

Achelluth, member of the Watch

Fush, sutler in the Renian army

Nazeed, one of Osiphan's conspirators

Phariayh, camp follower in the Renian army.

ONE:

AN EMPTY BANQUET

1

Vyissan awoke to the sun shining on his face, and struggled to open his eyes. Waves of pain assailed him, light and dark coruscating within his eyes. He worried for a moment that he was going to vomit from its intensity, but that feeling passed, resolving to a distant simmer in his stomach. He blinked until his eyes found a focus and the disparate floating shapes formed themselves into something coherent. Nothing looked familiar. He was unable to recall where he had last been or what had happened to him. He knew that he had been away, journeying, which explained his foreign surroundings, though little else.

He coughed and waited, but his mind failed to make sense of it, and eventually he simply got to his feet and began to look around. The room was quite spare, a bed and stand and a chair all that was present, the walls bare. He left it and found himself in a much larger room filled with book-lined shelves, a desk and a bureau and a table, all with heavy tomes on them as well. He felt a vague pang of familiarity and walked over to the desk to pick up one of the volumes, flipping it open at random. He looked over the lines of characters, the finest calligraphy, and while he could read all the words, it was not in his tongue.

Stepping outside, he found himself in a corridor that stretched off in one direction and went to a corner in the other. There was a painting on the far wall, a scene depicting the defense of a palace filled with red-shaded men. He studied it for a moment, but it meant nothing to him and he went down the hall, turning the corner to see what else there was. He had a clear sense that he was in a palace—the one depicted in the painting?—but no idea where that might be. The corridors twisted and turned, offering forks and junctions, but no feeling that he was headed to any particular place as he might have expected. It seemed like he must somehow have returned to his starting point in all his turnings, but he did not come to the painting again.

In fact, he realized, he had not passed any other paintings or tapestries in all his wanderings. There was nothing to orient him, for there were no windows, or even doors, and the corridors were unchanging. It was almost as if he were underground. A creeping panic started to seize him, the clawing of desperate fingers against a nailed tomb.

He started to move about the halls in a frenzy, his earlier pain forgotten, trying to grasp the design of the place. Just as he was about to despair ever finding his way out of this madhouse, he encountered Cepedutherupt idling at the end of one corridor, right at a point where it branched off again down three different avenues, one for each of the Gods. The High Adept nodded at his Disciple and gestured for him to follow, leading him down Ulternon's passage. Vyissan followed, nervous, feeling as though he shouldn't be in this place.

Cepedutherupt began to talk animatedly, glancing back to make sure Vyissan was listening. "These creatures, the Kragians, beyond fathoming. They do not submit to the natural laws of man. They are a menace to all civilization.

"The very fundamental meaning," he insisted to Vyissan, "of what we are lies in our ability to wrestle the alkemya, to wrestle astral from all things, by our own sweat, by our own being, not by some clattering hand. These creatures have no souls to send to Ulternon's Halls—oh, they profess belief, but it is a veneer, understand—and they would render all being soulless, the clattering of the machine."

He does not know who I am, Vyissan thought. *I am not who I am.* His hands, he saw, were stained red, and his face did not feel—it was not his own.

He awoke to the sun shining on his face, struggling to open his eyes. He wanted to gasp for air, though his breathing maintained its steady rhythm and finally he was able to will himself to a state of calm. The room he saw was the same one he had been in previously. It felt like he had been trapped in this bed for weeks, though he suspected it had only been a few days. There were vague memories of fever-ridden hours of sweating and shivering, carrying on insane monologues amidst the ministrations of his hosts. Nothing firm, though, not like the dream he had just emerged from. A vision, really. His hold on the real still felt tenuous, for this room, the sunlight and his breathing, none of it felt as alive as that.

He shivered and noticed a pitcher of water on the bedstand and struggled out of bed over to it. He was dizzy and weak from the work the poison had done on him, and as he tried to pour himself some water, he sent the cup crashing to the floor. A man in a grey robe came into the room at the sound, a look of stunned amazement on his face as he took in the sight of Vyissan leaning heavily against the bedstand, the shards of the cup littered at his feet. He shook his head and made a warding sign, backing out of the room as he did so.

A shout followed from the other room, and then he could hear someone being berated. He stayed where he was, desperate for water but unable to exert the energy needed to leave the room. Two men then entered. The man in the grey robe stood back near the doorway, as if he wanted to be ready to flee at a moment's notice. Vyissan thought him the curer, by the look of him and his clothes. The other man was Hasen, his guard, who approached him and led him back to the bed.

He found another cup and brought Vyissan some water. After he drank his fill, Hasen asked, "You are feeling well, Husem?"

Vyissan shrugged, clearing his throat. He spoke in a weak voice: "As well as might be expected. It was a powerful dose, whatever it was."

"Fyessen," the curer said, fear warring with revulsion in his voice. "No one can survive it once it is administered."

Vyissan nodded. "I'll consider myself lucky, then."

The curer muttered something underneath his breath and Hasen dismissed him curtly.

"The Vazeir has confided in me what you are. What you claim to be," he said quietly. "That is the only reason you can still be alive."

"Yes," Vyissan agreed. "What is this poison he mentioned?"

"Fyessen. There are few savants who know how to make it, something passed down from adept to disciple. If you know the right people in this city, you can buy it. I've heard that one of the bases is the poison glands of the gens frog, but there must be more than that, because in order to kill with that you would need to pierce the skin so the poison can enter the blood. Fyessen only needs to touch the skin and you are dead."

That explained the strangeness of the Ceinobyte's touch; it could not have been his flesh that had pressed against his forehead. The thought of the assassin brought him back to himself.

"Ahednar. A Ceinobyte," he said to the guard, who nodded grimly.

"You are all right?" Hasen asked.

Vyissan nodded. "Send some food when you have a chance."

Hasen clapped him on the shoulder and left him. Vyissan could hear him issuing instructions to the curer. For some reason it made him think of Cepedutherupt, and he wondered what the High Adept must be thinking given the long silence that had stretched between them these last days, however many there had been. It would wait, he thought, as the weight of exhaustion and pain that he had been working to fend off collapsed on him and he lay back down and went to sleep.

•••

It was a difficult business collecting an image and sending it over such a distance. The link between Disciple and Adept forged through months of meditation under the careful guidance of others in the Council was extremely tenuous, even for an Adept as powerful as Cepedutherupt. To effect the link, which normally, when they were no more than half a day's travel from each other, required little thought or effort, Vyissan had to reflect, searching for his balance, for over half an hour. Even then, his sense of the High Adept was nonexistent. If not for the almost immediate response, he might have believed that he was sending the image to hang over the vast skies of the desert, where some band of Shadows in their wandering might encounter it and wonder.

The images he received from the High Adept seemed as though they too had become lost for a time in their journey, pieces worn away by the elements of that harsh plain, the wind and the rock. He wondered if he was still feeling the ill effects of the poisoning, for he was incapable of drawing any sense from what he saw. He recognized the players: the Gver of Lastl, the Qraul, Attulliel of the Desu House and others. The meaning of it all, how they all fit together, kept slipping from his grasp, though he had the sense that he should know what the High Adept meant in showing him this. But the intrigues of the Qraul's Court seemed such a distant concern now that he was here in Vazeir's Palace in Darrhyn.

He shook himself uneasily and then rose from the table and decided to return to bed. Lying back with his eyes closed, but not yet slipping away to that peaceable oblivion, he thought of the strangeness of being a Disciple. That anyone of such capabilities and training should surrender his being to another, especially in those moments of communion where his very alkemy was Cepedutherupt's to do with as he chose, must be beyond all comprehension to anyone from outside the Council circle. He could only imagine what his hosts here would think if they knew. And perhaps they were right; perhaps Kercubegahedd had been correct in calling the Council Adepts slavers and the practice of Discipledom an abomination. He had to admit it had been a wonder to be free of the guiding hand, hovering behind his neck at all moments, these last weeks. He could have used his alkemya without question or regard, gone off and disappeared, never to be heard of again, with the High Adept helpless to do anything.

Vyissan was not Cepedutherupt's first Disciple, of course; there were at least two others that he knew of. The one previous to him had taken to bed three years ago, unable to perform his duties, and so had been released from Discipledom to live out his days. Vyissan had seen him shuffling about the Council quarters in Craitol, a wasted and bent form, looking, for all the Realm, like an elder, though he was no older than the High Adept himself.

The other had died in the war against Kercubegahedd. Not much was said of how it had happened, though Vyissan had heard that he had been transmuted to nothing, all his alkemy drawn from him, leaving only the flesh and nothing of the being within. It was one of the gravest crimes against the Council and its rule that could be imagined, if it were true. Vyissan thought it unlikely. Many were jealous of the High Adept and his standing.

He insisted on meeting the Vazeir in one of the outer rooms, and walked there under his own power. He could feel his strength returning, though it had only been a day since his fever had broken. When the Vazeir, came he accepted his offer of a quid, though the juice did not sit well in his stomach.

The Vazeir inquired politely after his health before turning to the matter at hand. "We have arrested Ahednar. He denies everything, of course. We couldn't find a trace of poison in the room, but only a fool would keep that around longer than necessary. We did find these, though."

He passed him some cloth pads, made from a fabric Vyissan did not recognize. They were the size of a fingertip and the shade of a Renian's skin.

"He had paste, too, so he could stick these to his fingers. And so."

"What about the poison touching his own skin, Husem?"

The Vazeir smiled. "The ones who make the poison make these as well. It is fair to say they know what they are about."

It seemed to Vyissan that the Vazeir knew a great deal on the subject as well, which he supposed was not surprising. Poisons were clearly in common use in the Empire, much more so than Craitol, where the Council had established some immunities.

"If I might intrude, Husem, has the Emperor made any decisions as yet? The glorious Qraul will be awaiting my word."

"Discussions have been put on hold," the Vazeir said. "Frankly, we were waiting to see if you came through. No one expected it, and the Ad Eselte assumed that would be the end of it, at least until another emissary could be sent to the court."

Before Vyissan could reply, the Vazeir called Hasen into the room. "We also found this among Ahednar's things ."

The guard carried an engine into the room and set it on the table between the two men. Vyissan did not even bother to disguise his surprise as he stared at its swirling tubes of quicksilver, sensing the latent astral in that liquid. He leaned away from it.

"How did he come to have this?"

"Ancestors know. We found it concealed in a statue of a bird. We have no idea what it is, though that must be quicksilver in it. And how it works." The Vazeir shrugged.

"It is quicksilver," Vyissan said.

"You know what it is?"

"I do. Destroy it."

He tried to summon some force to his voice, but it sounded empty to his ears. The Vazeir studied him carefully, his face betraying none of his thoughts, and he said nothing more.

2

The patter of the rain atop the cover of the palanquin formed an interminable rhythm that echoed within its confines and seemed to reverberate deep into Keleprai's being. He sighed and stretched out his legs, trying to ignore it. Keleprai felt damp even though the carriage was not leaking, the rain permeating even the empty air around him. He had come to the Lasisen Cloister to see Dalenna half an hour before, sending an attendant to the gate to ask entrance. To this point he had not returned. Keleprai very much wanted to find out what was going on, but he would not be seen leaving the palanquin to do so, especially in the midst of this deluge.

His mind and body both unoccupied, he could not resist picking through the events of the day before, those fateful hours. He had eaten at himself, gnawing deeper and deeper, leaving himself paralyzed and incapable of any decision. Not that it had mattered—every choice had been touched with disaster, from the moment he had sent Tehh's Disciple with the note to Byuvir.

Now the Veil was returned and blood would inevitably follow. It was not a time to be out of the Realm, in the desert chasing visions. He had known that, had said as much, and in the end he had done nothing. Madness. He was touched—not the Adepts; no, they always got what they desired when the cards were played and the coin was due. For all he knew Tehh and Cepedutherupt had conspired together, this end always in sight, leading him to this paralysis when he was the one person who might have ended this folly. He would put nothing past them.

He could not resist glancing across the palanquin to the bench where Kigarle sat, his face pinched and clouded with pallor, the only evidence of the wound he had received at the hands of the Veil's assassin. It had been such a near thing, the knife poised before his face, where Tehh's Disciple had paralyzed him, allowing young Donier the opportunity to be the hero. Kigarle had not been so lucky.

That he was here now was beyond belief. The thaumaturge who had attended to the wound had insisted on bed rest until the wound had closed over, but Kigarle had ignored him, insisting on attending to Keleprai while he saw to the High Adept's demands. He had been silent since they had left the Qraul's Palace, which was unlike him, and Keleprai feared that his injury was bothering him more than he let on. The Godsforsaken fool.

As he resisted the urge to give voice to his thoughts, the curtain to the carriage was drawn back and the attendant leaned his dripping head into the compartment.

"Most Gracious. They will not let us in without the say so of the Most Glorious Mother. They sent someone from the gate to the cloister, but he has not returned yet."

There was a question in the attendant's statement. Keleprai shrugged. "Then we wait his return."

The attendant inclined his head and closed the curtain to return to the gate. Keleprai cursed to the rain. Here, the day after his utter humiliation and abasement, when he had seen for himself truly what he was, he carried out the High Adept's bidding. Or attempted to do so, only to be thwarted by Dalenna. Word was she saw no one but her son. Who was the Godsforsaken fool?

It had been at least two years since he had seen her. She had not come with the rest of the court the year before when the Qraul had visited Lastl. Maybe not since the Qraul's wedding day. It was strange to think, for she had been so present in his thoughts these last weeks, filling his nights with her wanderings, disappearing during the daylight hours, leaving him to wonder why he could not rid her from his mind.

No, it had been two years before when his court had come to pay obeisance to the Qraul. He recalled that she had departed the celebration that evening after the invocations were spoken, a sign then of her growing devotion to the path of the Gods. He had been surprised, and had remarked on it to Kigarle, who was standing with him just beyond the Qraul's circle.

"She never struck as the sort to bar the door to her palace," Kigarle had said. "I always thought she was willing to have a drudge to do his labor, provided the gate was left closed."

Keleprai had shrugged and Kigarle had continued, "Such a beauty, though. But you know the sort. Love is a game and she holds all the trumps, and will play them."

He looked at his friend now and saw a ripple of pain cross his face. "A fool's errand, this," he said, with a thin smile.

Kigarle tried to smile in turn, but it was more of a grimace, marred by his discomfort. "Aren't they all?" he said, his voice sounding weak.

"Some more than others."

"What is the High Adept's desire in this?" Kigarle said, closing his eyes as he shifted in his seat.

The rain surged and roared outside. "He fears she will turn the boy against him and this path."

"What matter is that?" Kigarle said, his voice cadaverous. "The ardehs have been yoked, the wheels are already turning. Not even the Qraul himself could stop this now."

Keleprai nodded. It was true. Why, then, was he here? Had the whims and machinations of the Gods led him astray to their own obscure purpose? Why did the High Adept want him here on this day? What was being done while he was securely occupied on this fool's errand?

A chill rippled down his spine and he shivered deeply. The man had been acting strangely since the Council, his long-sought-after triumph secured, and yet he had been almost morose, worried about some far-distant thing which he would not give word to in Keleprai's presence. The threat of the Veil—a second assassination attempt, with more surely to follow—Cepedutherupt had dismissed with a wave of his hand, as if it were of no account. Glancing over at Kigarle, who was barely masking his agony, Keleprai well knew it was of account. Blood had been spilled, pain suffered, and there was the promise of more to be endured, yet all the High Adept cared for was to go to the desert and chase Shadows.

Or to bring the mother of the Qraul to heel to no purpose. A thousand conspiracies played through Keleprai's head, reasons for this absurd game, all to ensure his compliance in this madness. The secrets of the Realm were at last revealed to him. He chewed his lip a moment and pulled aside the curtain and stuck his head out into the rain. He had to yell three times before the attendant heard and came from the gate, where Keleprai told him that they were returning to the Qraul's Palace.

3

Masiph read the note for tenth time in the last minute. There was no doubt as to its provenance, though it had been sent in an anonymous pouch and was unsealed and unsigned. The scent was unmistakable, though he was still not able to place what its ingredients were. A concoction of her own, he thought, echoing what Lisser had said to him, and that led him to thoughts of the dead merchant and the bite on his ear, the scab yet to heal over completely.

The note consisted of one line, drawn by an elegant hand with formal characters: *Need is desire with the blade out, longing at its bloody point.* He wondered if she might have taken it from the writings of some Sage, but he decided it was unlikely. It lacked a certain elegance, though there were many who certainly would not hesitate to warn of the corrupting power of need. He could not make sense of what she meant by it, either. Was she referring to her own need, or mocking his? The latter more likely, letting him know that his desire would carry a price and she would be the one to name it. And he would pay.

"Come," he called to a knock at the door, expecting to see his eunuch Ctuellen. Instead Ibrazol stepped within, closing the door quietly behind him. He looked around Masiph's sitting room and frowned a bit in distaste, taking in the remains of the day's meals on the table, as well as the scattered refuse of his existence. There were a few ceremonial daggers with bejeweled sheaths he had spent too much coin on, never to wear, various parts of robes that had

14

somehow escaped his bedchambers, and assorted trinkets he had acquired in his wanderings through the markets which had interested at the moment but that he had put aside as soon as he returned to his quarters.

He jumped to his feet, nearly setting his chair over as he did. "Father," he said, for lack of anything else.

Ibrazol nodded and sat at the table, gesturing for Masiph to do the same. They faced each other in awkward silence, Ibrazol seeming to collect his thoughts—to what end, Masiph could not guess. It had to be something significant that would draw him from the palace, where he had spent nearly all his time these last weeks. That Ibrazol might have made the journey specifically to speak with him was terrifying to contemplate. To make matters worse, he could not stop looking at the woman's note, which lay between them on the table, open for the reading.

He stood up abruptly and asked Ibrazol if he would like to take some wine. Receiving a nod of assent, he went over to the counter where he had put the half-finished bottle from his dinner, and fumbled about for two cups, thanking his ancestors that there were actually two that happened to be clean. He poured them each a cup, setting the bottle between them, and then cleaned off the table of its miscellany, including, to his utter relief, the letter. When he had settled himself again, Ibrazol was ready to speak.

"There is a matter on which I need to speak with you." Masiph thought for a moment he was going to faint. He was certain he was about to be disowned. That was the best outcome; there was every chance his father would turn him over to the Imperial Guard.

"What I'm about to say stays with us. It does not leave this room." He paused as though he were debating whether he should continue. "We will be going to war in the desert."

"Against the Shadow Men?" Masiph could not help himself.

"Yes," his father replied, the curtness in his voice suggesting he was not to be interrupted again. "And it will be soon. This season. There is obviously a great deal I cannot tell you, but there is no doubt of it going forward. I think you know what this means."

Masiph did not dare say one way or the other.

"We will need to call up all our forces. You will be elevated. I have spoken with Gheyuth, and he has promised me that you will have a good unit. You will be going to battle. Do your ancestors proud."

All this was said with only a trace of emotion. Masiph swallowed, still unsure what he should say.

"We will have to talk of your marriage as well. It should be arranged for you when you return."

"Of course," Masiph said quietly. He bit his tongue to stop himself from smiling, the wave of exultation rising within him almost overwhelming.

Ibrazol rose to his feet, downing his wine in a gulp. "This is good for our family, ancestors smile upon us.

"Remember," he said, turning as he left the room, "on your life, this stays in this room."

The last was said with such menace that Masiph wondered just what his father did know. As quickly as it had come, his excitement disappeared, replaced by a clenched feeling somewhere between fear and anger. He told himself to be calm—after all, he had gotten all he wanted, in spite of whatever Ibrazol might suspect or know. But it was an empty satisfaction, for he could not shake the question of why, after so long, he was being given this chance.

4

Keleprai a Lastl was the last of the Gvers to take his leave of Qraul's Court and return to his city to begin preparations for the coming war. Most of the Gvers left in haste without ceremony, for there was little time for them to gather their forces and begin the march to Takyl, where the army would assemble for the Qraul to lead them into the desert. Already the Enir mercenary companies were beginning to arrive, camping on the outskirts of the capital after their journey from the Republics up the river. The Qraul's army had been summoned from their barracks, and spent the mornings in training and the afternoon in parades throughout the city, thronged by the populace, who cheered them on for at last striking at the scourge of the desert.

Alieren watched these developments, alternating between fury and despondence. How arrogant of the High Adept to believe he would win the day at the Council of Gvers, and how right he had been. That she, as Qraulla of the Realm, was forced to endure many of these parades, where each exultant cry seemed to land like a blow, as well as to see each night the exuberant delight of her husband, only further befouled her mood.

The only thing that gave her some satisfaction was to see that Cepedutherupt shared none of Laterala's delight at his carefully engineered triumph. His face was lined with worry, the multitude of preparations for his grand adventure now suddenly upon him, and the reality of what he had done and the cost of failure should it come weighing fully upon him. Keleprai, too, before he had left for

Lastl, had been a shadow of his usual self, barely speaking to the High Adept or Laterala, not even embarrassing himself with the dancers.

The days that followed were even stranger for Alieren, filled with the frenzy of planning and organization, absent of the usual ceremony that filled her hours. Worst of all, she found herself missing that tedium, the empty moments almost too much to bear, with only thoughts of her own failure and the empty weeks to come to worry at her mind. For with Laterala and the army would go most of the Qraul's Court, leaving only Elihaun, Master of Offices, to rule her days. Nominally, of course, she was to hold court in her husband's absence, but Elihaun and the High Adept would see that he remained her guiding hand. A thoroughly unlikeable man, made more so by the fact that he clearly despised her. She was but a northerner, not worthy of the court, the city or the Qraul.

Every day he seemed to find the words to unsettle and provoke her, all couched in his bureaucratic niceties.

"Your complexion seems poor today, Most Glorious Qraulla," he said, as he was announced by Geylin, her lady in waiting, into her audience chamber to bring her the day's tasks. Geylin stood by the door, a protection of her noble virtue. "Perhaps it is a sign you are at last with child."

Her failure to provide an heir for Laterala was a further mark against her in his mind, one that he never failed to remind her of when the opportunity presented itself.

"A happy thought," she said, keeping her voice even. She had long ago learned that it was no good to allow herself to be provoked by him; it just served to give him further arms to strike at her with.

Elihaun stared at her with an expression of stone, as though searching her words for mockery. Alieren met his gaze steadily. She had long given up hope of Laterala providing her with an heir. How many trulls had he lain with in the years since they had been married? And not one of them had borne a child by him. No matter the insinuation and the disapproval of Elihaun, the High Adept and their many courtiers and servants, it was all too clear where the fault lay.

Part of her wanted to look Elihaun in the eye and say, "If you truly want an heir, dismiss your eunuch watchers and I will call in my guard and see what they can provide me." The thought alone was enough to make her smile. Elihaun responded with his own thin-lipped disapproving smile that made her want to shudder with revulsion.

"There are long and trying days ahead for you, Most Immortal," he said. "The absence of the glorious Qraul will be like a wound."

"For him as well," Alieren said. That Laterala had come to care for her in his way, and more importantly to trust her, was, she thought, the only thing that to this point had halted any attempts by the Master of Offices and the High Adept to dissolve the marriage they had crafted.

"Yes, of course, Most Gracious," Elihaun said. "But he shall be seeing to the glory of the Realm. That should ease the ache in his heart."

"As will my duties here. I am certain I will be kept busy," Alieren said, raising an eyebrow to let him know she wanted no part of being his compliant performer and reading his lines. The Master of Offices blinked, though his careful mask remained in place. How he despised her.

"If he were to return and find that a child was expected, it would truly be a gift from the Gods," he said, leaning toward her. She made it a point never to allow him to sit in her presence. He allowed her no ease with his eunuch spies and constant barbs, so she would grant him none as well.

"I can only pray Melinon will bless me," she said, and rose to her feet, going to stand near the balcony that overlooked her private garden, staring down at the flowers in bloom, her back to him. Why was he here, she wondered, if not to discuss her audiences at court for the day, with Laterala attending to the army, the training in courtly practice he had insisted on these last days for the day, soon to come, when the army would march for the desert. Yet he seemed in no hurry to do so this day.

"But I fear I am keeping you from your duties," she said, turning back to him.

"Not at all, Most Gracious," he said, a poisonous smile seizing his lips. "My duty is to you, especially in the days to come. But I bring word that the army and Our Glorious Qraul departs in two days."

"Thank you for your kindness," she said. She had known the day was coming, but it still seemed impossible that it could be here so soon. Cepedutherupt had spoken of weeks of preparation being needed before the Council Adepts would be ready to go forth with the army, which was still being assembled. She tried not to let the sudden despair she felt show on her face.

"Have no fear, Most Gracious," he said, the malicious smile still spreading across his face. "He will return to your bed tonight, to see if he can get you with child before he goes."

Alieren went cold at his blunt words. This was a change. Would more be forthcoming once Laterala was gone?

"If a blessing does not appear," he continued, "something will have to be done."

He bowed deeply and took his leave without waiting for a word from her. She felt weak in the knees, and had to move quickly to sit down. Geylin rushed from the door to her side, but Alieren waved her away. She put a hand to her temple and bit her tongue, trying to ward off the terror that had her stomach churning.

Elihaun was threatening her with the dissolution of her marriage and her exile to the north. It would be the end of her family's standing among the Craitolian nobles. Even the northern families would turn aside from them. And what would become of her, if it happened?

She cursed Cepedutherupt and his mad war with the Shadows. It would be Laterala's ruin, she was certain, as well as her own. She could only hope it would be the High Adept's as well.

5

Donier returned to Lastl a hero, the protector of the Gver, his future and his family's rise in rank assured. Yet what should have been his greatest triumph, a feast for his soul, was poisoned by the knowledge that the Golden Veil remained lurking in the shadows. They would return to him again, knowing that the further his star rose, the more closely he would be bound to them, needing to pay for their confidence. And pay he would, for he could not desecrate his family's hopes by allowing such knowledge to come to light. Even though it would, he knew that with certainty as well. There would come a point where the Veil would have no further use of him and they would plunge the knife into his throat.

That he would have no time to savor his new status, given he would be going to war in the desert in a matter of days, did not help his outlook on matters. Deepening his misery was Ulrien's refusal to return with him to Lastl. Gver Keleprai had awarded him thirty gold coins for saving his life—the fact that he had been at least partially responsible for placing the Gver in such danger in the first place was an irony Donier did not indulge much thought in—and he had offered to use it to arrange for quarters for Ulrien on Concubine Row. Such a fortune would be enough to keep her well for several years there.

But she had declined his offer, saying, "Oh, I could never leave Craitol. It is my home."

He had been stunned, unable really to comprehend what she was saying. What trull turned down a well-appointed apartment and a steady wage with a noble of rank? "Do I displease you?" he had managed to say. "Were the hours we spent together so unhappy?"

"Oh no," she said, wide-eyed, placing her hand upon his. "It is not that at all. The nights were wonderful, and I would love to have more with you. But I cannot leave this city. I am sorry to disappoint you."

There had been nothing else to say. He would not humiliate himself further by asking her again, no matter how he much he wanted to. He had taken his leave and tried to put her from his mind, so far without success. The hot and dusty highway from Craitol to Lastl had offered little succor, and though the preparations for war were consuming, his thoughts still strayed to Ulrien at the first instance of idleness.

His evenings were free of her specter, but that was only because of the dreams which continued to harass him. Even on those Gods-blessed nights when they did not visit him, his sleep was uneasy and he too often chased himself to wakefulness in his fear at their possible arrival. He began to sink into a heavy stupor during the day, dragging at his thoughts and actions as he plied the realms of light. As he and Ludenn made the preparations for their cohort to journey to Takyl and beyond, he would catch himself staring off into the distance as the rest of the cohort moved around him, unable to recall what he was doing, in his eyes the empty desert sky, the sun's rays like knives.

He made a point, before the cohort left for Takyl, to call on Liene. It had been weeks since he had seen her. One burden too many, with the dreams and his own problems with the Veil occupying his thoughts. There had been nothing to tell her anyway, at least nothing that offered hope. No sign of Terainous had been found, to the surprise of no one, though nothing was really done, and the Afusel remained steadfast in their refusal to acknowledge his death. Liene's dowry was still in dispute as a result, and she was unable to leave the Afusel estates without being accused of abandoning her marriage.

Visiting her was like going to the Gerunil to speak to the men of rank imprisoned there. The sense of dissipation on the estate grew more apparent with each visit he made, as did Liene's plainly growing despair at ever being free of the place. He was always brought to the same room that looked out onto the courtyard, the same servant standing watch, and, in spite of the open windows and the light, he still felt as though he was enclosed in some low-ceilinged room where the air could not move and mold crept up the walls.

The last he had heard of her was from a family friend, who had mentioned that she had taken to bed with some mysterious illness. Recalling the Feast of Balance at the Gver's Palace, Donier had wondered about the nature of that illness. *To think I saved that man,* he told himself, *when he does not bother to lift a finger for a woman he has bedded.* And yet, what had he done? Little more, and to no effect.

The question of whether Terainous was still alive or not had gone to the courts, but it would be months, perhaps a year, before any conclusion would come from that. And if, as everyone expected, the Afusel lost, they could appeal and appeal, to the Gver, even, delaying any resolution in their mad quest to maintain the dowry lands for as long as possible. Such was their state that even the embarrassment of a public court battle that they could not conceivably hope to win was worth it to extract the windfall of one more harvest from the lands she had brought to the marriage.

He had arranged ahead of time to call on the estate, and when he arrived they brought him to the same room. Liene was waiting for him, sitting in the same chair she always did, but it was clear she was not well. Her face was pale, the flesh gone from it, the body beneath her dress a protrusion of bones settled on the chair. It was clear she should not have been sitting—her breathing was shallow and labored, and she struggled to keep herself upright.

Seeing her that way, all her beauty gone, the vivacious red of her skin gone sallow, was too much. He stared at the ever-present servant with accusing eyes. The man returned his gaze without emotion, waiting for this duty to be finished.

She did not meet his eyes, did not answer any questions; the only sound escaping her lips was the passing of her breath. He tried some pleasant jokes, some encouraging laughter, and spoke confidently of the successful conclusion of the issue in the courts. It was all a lie, and eventually he tired of the burden of maintaining it and took his leave.

He put her from his mind as best he could, an easier task these days with his troubled soul and the complicated state of his own affairs. He kept expecting to see Uherl materialize before him when he was walking the streets, but he never did. The cohort's preparations continued until the day Ludenn's messenger arrived at his estate to inform Donier that they would be leaving for Takyl the next day. The Qraul was on the march from Craitol.

At times he wondered if maybe the realms were crumbling together, a conflagration without end, the Gods abandoning their idle children to their fate—for what other explanation was there for these black days?

6

The robes were crisp and new and they settled over him easily. The loose inner layer was of ardeh wool stained red, like his uniforms on the Watch. The outer layer, though, was of a high-quality Craitolian silk, a vibrant green. Nustef slipped the armor over his head, enjoying its weight on his shoulders. Just wearing it left him trembling with excitement. He moved the handglass up and down to get the full effect, and was quite pleased with what he saw. A shield and a spear and he would be a soldier in more than just name.

He set the glass down and went to find Erise. She wasn't in the main room of their quarters, so he took off the armor and stepped outside to the hallway, walking out to the balcony overlooking the courtyard. The sun had almost disappeared and someone had already lit the lamps in the courtyard, making the overcast twilight less grim. The shouts of children at play below echoed up to him. Erise was sitting on a bench by herself chewing a quid, staring dully below. He paused for a moment, wincing to himself. Their ancestors had failed to bless them with children, something he knew pained her deeply.

He walked up beside her, leaning against the balcony, and then pointed at his robes with a flourish. She looked them over, her expression vacant, and then turned her gaze back to the atrium.

He felt a rush of anger stinging his cheeks. "What?" he said, stopping himself from saying anything more.

She did not look at him. "You'll forgive me," she said slowly, "if

I don't get excited about this madness. There isn't much to get excited about, so far as I'm concerned."

"Why not? You know what this means to us."

"I know what it means to you."

He bit off a reply before he spoke, and tried to contain his anger. It was the children below, he told himself, that had set her in this mood. That was her only desire; she could not fathom his need, his ambition to find his way to a new life when what they had now was more than she had ever had.

"You know I don't trust that Nohritai," she said. "He is nothing more than a spoiled child. Never spent a day where he didn't know where his meals were coming from. Never a want."

Nustef let that pass. One chose one's battles, after all. And there was truth, he had to admit, to what she said, though it was only a part. How could she know the rest, though?

"He's using you," she added with authority.

"How can he be using me?" Nustef asked in disbelief.

"How often have you spoken in the last months? He only sends for you when he has nothing better to do, don't you see? When you were in the Watch he liked you because you treated him decently, and everyone else couldn't be bothered to respect some High Nohritai's son playing at soldiering. And now he's in the army, a jetthir again, of course, and he's worried the same thing will happen, that his men will see him for what he is. So he wants you there, for someone who will treat him well no matter if he deserves it.

"You are too good a man. This is a game for him. He'll dabble in this for a while, and then when he's ready to move on to something new, his father will arrange it. And you..."

She let her words hang, nothing more needing saying. Their eyes met in the flickering twilight and held fast, the silence that embraced them seeming to spread outward, pressing against the courtyard.

"This is a good thing," he said, hoping his voice was firmer than it sounded to him. "There's more pay in the army, more prestige. If everything goes well, I'll be a jetthir in a few years. And once that happens, who's to say how far I might go? I have a name, after all."

She turned and put the remainder of her quid in the spittoon by the bench. He watched her, a feeling of helplessness stealing over him.

"I never would have gotten in on merit," he said, and it was a hard thing to admit.

"You don't know that," she said immediately. "It is a shaved die."

"All life is, ancestors provide."

She looked away from him back to the courtyard and the settling darkness. He was acutely aware of all the noise around them, all the families in their quarters, their windows and doors flung open, chatter and cries and moans scattering out. He listened to it for a moment, letting it wash over him, staring up at the sky, the dark, looming clouds outlined by the remnants of the now-disappeared sun.

"The colors suit you," Erise said, and he smiled. She looked away, unable to meet his eyes, and he put his arm around her.

Erise settled in against him. "I bought this for you," she said, handing him a small neckerchief of the sort that travelers wore in the desert to protect their faces from the wind. It was a peacock blue, a lucky color.

"Wear it and bring it back to me," she said.

"I will," Nustef said.

She ran her hand along his arm, playing the silk between her fingers. "I already feel parched from the lack of you to come. It will be the fasting of our souls."

"I know. I fear how great my appetite will grow while I am gone with no cellar to store my root."

She elbowed him. "Be sure to stay away from stews and prunes. One is too light, the other too sweet."

Nustef laughed. "I've no need of such poor sustenance. I'm made of sterner stuff. Besides, there is sweet enough on my plate here."

"My heart breaking and you talk of me so. Maybe I'll grow used to your absence."

"I never will. I'll hold thoughts of you fast to me. You'll be the blossoming tree that I cling to in that desolate place."

"I hope that my tree bears fruit," Erise said, and he followed her gaze to where the children played below.

"Yes," he said. "You are a fine tree, bearing a sweet harvest. Ancestors willing, we shall share it."

She stood, loosing herself from his arms, and led him with her back into their quarters.

"We'll find our way somehow," she said.

"Yes," Nustef said, kissing her.

"I'll keep my fruit ready for when you return," she said, her hands upon her dress and then his robes.

"And when I return?"

"A supper. No, a banquet," she said, laughter in her voice.

"A feast from a bountiful harvest."

7

The army left Darrhyn two days before Duihherin, the seventh Ad Eselte's day, as an afternoon storm erupted overhead. The streets leading from the barracks to the Desert Gate were lined with a cheering throng as people from all districts came to show their support for this battle against the endless scourge that had blighted so many of their lives and their ancestors. Nohritai ladies, hidden behind curtained palanquins, had their servants throw the petals of desert flowers at the departing soldiers, who caught them and put them on their shields.

The entire capital had been in a frenzy of anticipation for this moment once word had come that war was to be made. Even news of the strange alliance with the Qraul of Craitol had not dampened the fervor. If they could deal the Shadows a mortal blow, and many were suddenly convinced that they could, then the raids which had marked their entire lifetimes with fear would perhaps dwindle to a minor concern, by ancestors' grace.

It was enough that, after a season that had seen more than its share of awful events perpetrated upon the Empire—whether by the Shadows or others—the Ad Eselte was striking a blow, forcing the Shadow Men to face the sword. After nearly a hundred years of retreat and seemingly intractable decline, to be setting forth against the Shadow Men was a satisfying thing. It was at last, so many said, a day to be proud.

Masiph id Ezern marched at the head of his quadra, Nustef at his side, through the city gates, erect and proud, his heart soaring as it never had before. After so many years having his hopes denied, his dreams ignored by his father, it seemed impossible to believe that he was here on the precipice of a monumental journey that would define all his years to come, just as the work he was doing would help to create the Empire to follow. Perhaps this, he allowed himself to think, was the cusp of the moment when all their fortunes turned and they could return to the desert, seizing it from the Shadow Men's grasp.

If ancestors favored, all would go well and his descendants would be invoking his name for the deeds he achieved in this place. The thought delighted him. That he was favored could not be denied. He had survived a gruesome injury at the hands of the Shadow Men, a singular event, and had escaped without apparent consequence from the folly of Osiphan's insurrection.

Not entirely escaped, his purse was considerably lighter, and he would have to do without his jetthir's kenir, the twenty coins given each jetthir to help allay the cost of provisioning their journey across the desert. It would be a hardship, for it meant he would have to keep his robes himself, and perhaps go without wine or companionship at some point during the journey, for he would be expected, as jetthir, to show some largess toward his quadra, paying for feasts or their share of drink at various points during their march. To not do so would leave him open to mutiny from his men, who already no doubt saw him as a pretender, the unfavored son of the Imperial Vazeir.

The coin he had given to the woman. She had sent him a series of notes, all fragments of verse involving daggers and blood stirred, among other less-than-appealing imagery, until finally he determined to call on her again, returning to the anonymous quarters where she had first taken him. A man with an ugly scar across his nose answered the door, raising an eyebrow in question at Masiph's presence on the threshold.

"I am here to see her," Masiph said, holding up the latest of her missives, her elusive scent still heavy upon it.

The man grunted, blinking at the letter he clearly could not read, and shrugged.

"I wish to speak with her," Masiph said, returning the letter to his robes.

The man shrugged again, as though what Masiph suggested were impossible.

"I will not leave until I have spoken to her."

This at last moved the scarred man to speak in a voice heavy with phlegm. "You can stay long as you want. She ain't here."

"Where is she, then? I need to speak with her. Our present situation cannot be allowed to continue."

This earned him another shrug, and the man began to close the door.

"Wait," Masiph said, stepping forward so that he was blocking the door. "I am willing to pay for her silence."

Another shrug and the man held out his open palm, his expression unchanged.

"I will not give it to you," Masiph said, unable to keep his frustration from his voice. "I will speak to her. We will come to an agreement. Then I will pay her."

"She won't see the likes of you," the man said, still holding his palm out.

"She will if she wants her coin." The man shrugged as if to say that Masiph would be the one accepting the consequences of that decision. "What are you, her counsel keeper?"

"She is her own."

"Then you are in her service?"

The man shrugged ambiguously and turned around, pulling back his robe to reveal the nape of his neck, which was marked by the same thin tribal scars that Masiph had seen on the woman. Were they lovers, then, he wondered, feeling jealousy surge in his blood. No matter; it proved beyond a doubt they were in league. Unable to bear the man's presence any longer, Masiph pulled out the purse which held his jetthir's kenir and slapped it into the man's palm.

"I leave for the desert in two days. This should buy her silence, at least until after I have returned."

The man shrugged, which Masiph took as his assent, and he turned on his heels and walked away from the place.

The thought of the debacle caused him to flush with embarrassment; it had all been so humiliating, a reminder of his utter stupidity since the night of his injury. He glanced at Nustef, resplendent in his green and red, a blue kerchief knotted about his throat, and smiled, telling himself not to dwell upon the matter any further.

"Have you ever had a more glorious day?" he said.

TWO:

ADEPTS AND FAMILIARS

8

Fush was sweating feverishly, sitting in the meager shade provided by the flap of his tent. A dull breeze stirred the tent, providing modest relief from the heat, though it died almost as soon as it had begun. Phariayh could feel his gaze upon her as she bent to scour the pot that had been used to prepare the morning's porridge of maize, but which someone had neglected to clean, and had to resist a shudder. She could only hope one of the sulihers, preferably one of the Husems with a little coin to spend, took a fancy to her tonight so that she did not have to spend it beneath the sutler's damp and fleshy body. Though, judging by the growing darkness of his face, as well as his labored breathing, he might not have the energy for such efforts two nights in a row.

"A little faster with the pots, dear Phariayh," Fush called out. "There is still the robes to see to."

"Yes master," she said, without a glance back, not bothering to quicken her pace. Unlike him, she had walked the day's march, not been carried in a palanquin by slaves, and could feel exhaustion beginning to work at her edges, though her day's work had only just begun.

The days ahead promised to be hard. Breaking camp in the dim light before dawn and marching behind the army, setting camp in the evening and then doing a day's work in an evening, followed by the briefest of respites before beginning again. There were hundreds like her, men and women, slaves and indentured servants, the army's shadow, as they were called. Those who fed the sulihers, mended their wounds and robes, repaired their weapons and shared their beds. All for a price, paid to men like Fush, who grew fat on the misery of war.

She finished with the pot and turned to Fush, who looked it over and nodded his approval. "See to the robes," he said. "When they are ready, take them to the quadra and see if one of them will take you tonight." He did not sound confident in her chances.

"Yes, master," she said, scurrying by him into the tent to find the robes. Though she was free from the sun's rays within, the air was still, the heat festering, and she felt sweat began to pool in her armpits and on her back.

"Here." One of the other girls handed her a suliher's woolen inner robe, which had worn thin at the shoulder. A cheap and shoddily made thing, she saw, patched over many times.

As she set about to mend it, she glanced over at the girl, who was busy with her own robe. Phariayh could not recall her name; there were too many of them in Fush's keep, most newly acquired, only indentured with him a week or so, for the Ad Eselte's war declaration had been very late in coming. She herself had been bought the day before the army had been due to march, Fush desperate for any woman with a little training who was healthy enough to keep up with an army on the march. He had not wanted her, but the markets had been empty of good slaves or good servants whose debts could be purchased. She had been the best of a poor lot and he had taken her, paying the price asked and telling the slaver, "I will make no coin from her."

The girl frowned when she saw Phariayh staring at her, and she looked away, embarrassed. None of the girls had said anything to her, beyond what needed to be said in the course of their duties. The sulihers all looked at her warily, muttering to themselves as she passed by. She knew why: she had mark of the demon upon her, the tinge of darkness that said she had Shadow Men in her blood.

Their reactions did not surprise her, though; she was used to them by now. Her singular shade had been a burden her entire life. She had been abandoned by her mother to the care of Ceinobytes at a sanctuary just beyond the city walls of Darrhyn. In her mind she could imagine her mother holding this child, which so clearly illustrated the foul congress she had engaged in to the world, and being unable to bear the accusing eyes of everyone she met. Phariayh understood; she had to bear those same eyes, her mother's crime now her own.

She often wondered what the circumstance of her creation had been. Had her mother, whom she always saw as a pure light-shaded olive green, as the Nohritai in Darrhyn often looked, been ravished during a Shadow Men raid? Or had she been an indentured servant who had sought illicit pleasure in the arms of a Shadow Man slave? Or perhaps she was, as some of the songs went in drinkeries late at night, a pure-shaded Nohritai lady who had given in to her terrible desires and fornicated with one of her father's slaves. The pregnancy would have been hidden, her mother cloistered away in the family's estate, and the shameful progeny would have been snatched from her hands and taken to the women's sanctuary, where none were turned away.

She was not sure why the specifics of her origin mattered exactly, the end result was still the same. She would have been raised in the sanctuary regardless, forced to earn her keep there by the sisters as soon as she was able, to pay the debt she had incurred. But it did matter to her—it was the last thing she thought on those bleakest days before she drifted off to sleep, that somehow her Nohritai-born mother had freed herself from the clutches of her family and had come searching for the daughter she had lost and would free her from this miserable existence. A terrible fantasy to indulge in, given she knew it could never happen, and yet it was the only thing that offered any solace to her.

When they were done with the repairs on the robes, Phariayh and the other girl took them out to the quadra to give to the soldiers, along with that evening's meal, a stew of chicken and squash. While Phariayh ladled out servings of the stew to each of the sulihers, the girl gave back the robes and collected coins to pay for the meal. Each man had to pay from his own purse, and Phariayh could hear them muttering to each other about the miserliness of their jetthir, a high-born Nohritai, no less, who had yet to pay for a meal on their journey and had given no sign that he ever would.

After the bread and stew had been distributed, the girl sat among the soldiers as they ate, flirting and laughing, laying a hand on an arm or knee, trying to entice them into spending a little more coin for a night in her arms. Phariayh stood on the edge of the loose circle of sulihers, clutching the empty pot of stew, desperately willing one of them to cast an inviting eye toward her so that she might be spared another evening with Fush, though she had little urge to have their rough hands about her. She did not dare join them as the girl had, for even as she had dished out their meal, she could feel their dark stares, daggers upon her back.

It was the girl who finally took notice of her, glancing up from where she sat on the lap of one of the sulihers. "What are you still doing here?" she said, spitting the words at Phariayh. "That pot will not clean itself. And none of these men will lie with a demon cunt like yours."

Her harsh words elicited guffaws from the men, and Phariayh ran away, almost stumbling in the growing shadows of the dusk in her haste to be gone. She picked her way among the various quadras spread out along the narrow valley the imperial highway had taken them upon, using the fires to guide her to the sutler's tent near the back of the encampment.

When he saw her returning with the pot, the darkness not yet having taken hold, he shook his head. "The coin I spent on you is lost. I should have known better than to purchase someone so ugly. See to the pot, and when you are done, come to me. You will pay what you owe me one way or another."

Phariayh nodded meekly, not daring to look at him lest her revulsion show on her face, and set to work cleaning the pot. When she was done, she stood and watched the dying embers of the sun as it slipped behind the hills, so distant on this vast landscape. She had never felt so utterly alone, though she could hear hundreds of voices around her, could see some of the other girls returning from their assignations to sleep or finish the day's work. Seeing them reminded her that her toil was not yet complete, and she turned to go to the tent where Fush awaited her.

As she did, she saw a man cross in front of the sutler's tent, heading for the outskirts of the army's encampment. He was an Enir, judging by his beard, a strange sight in the Renian army, and she watched him pass by with some curiosity, wondering why he was here and what he was doing now. He sensed her watching him and turned to look her over, and she could see that he was taken aback by the sight of her shade, evident even with the failing light. Unlike so many others who would have spit upon the ground or made a sign against evil, he simply looked at her with the same curiosity she had felt for him.

For a moment she thought he would speak, but then he gave a

curt nod, more to himself than to her, and passed on beyond the camp and out of sight. Phariayh watched the shadows where he had vanished before turning back to the sutler's tent and the darkness that awaited her there.

9

They were put to a hard pace, Gheyuth, Vazeir of the Army, wanting to reach Esyln as soon as possible. That Duihherin was upon them meant the rainy season was ending and harvest and winter would be coming. Travel across the desert in the dry season, when rivers disappeared and game migrated north, was a hardship best not endured. At the Empire's height a journey to Esyln would take ten days for an army on the march. Only a few expeditionary forces had been on the road in the last few years, none daring to go as far as the jewel of the desert, so it was anyone's guess as to how good the highway would be farther on. And who was to say what ravages the desert might visit upon them?

To say nothing of the Shadow Men, who were everywhere in the desert, following no roads. In meetings with the jetthirs, Husem Gheyuth had said they would likely be attacked in the evening, while camp was being set, or before dawn, when most of the army would still be asleep. Meeting a large force seemed unlikely; it was not the Shadows' way. But they encountered no Shadow Men the first day of their journey. There were no attempts to attack the encamped army and there was no sign that they were even watched by the Shadows as they went.

On the second day it was Masiph's quadra that was chosen to lead the march, with he and Nustef leading scouting forays into the surrounding hills to see if there were any Shadows lurking. The day was hot, the vast sky empty but for the scouring sun. Here, well beyond the Eresnan River valley, the vegetation was sparse, mostly scrub and squat cactus plants that spread along the ground in odd segments, like the joints of bones badly set. When they stood atop a hill they could cast their gaze for miles in any direction, the horizon seemingly endless and as bare as the sky.

This, Masiph thought, as he stood marveling at the incredible distance, the almost overwhelming absence that seemed to dwarf him where he stood more than any mountain might, was the desert. The place of so many of his dreams, so near to where he had spent his entire life, and yet now that he was here he realized that it was an utterly foreign realm. He shivered with excitement, feeling the touch of his ancestors upon his neck.

A shout from one of his men, Yuluir, if Masiph remembered correctly, drew him from his thoughts, and he ran to the next rise to join the suliher. Yuluir was not standing on another of the rolling hills of the desert plain, as it had appeared from Masiph's vantage, but on a ridge overlooking a valley. There was a precipitous slope, almost impassable, dropping from the ridge to the depths below, heavy with rock and rust-colored earth. Yuluir was pointing into the valley depths and Masiph, following his line of sight, saw them, darkened specks on the red landscape, moving on the run.

"There's the demons, Husem," Yuluir said. "Already running, and we haven't even shown them our spears."

He thrust his hips as he said it, and laughed. Masiph forced a smile to his lips, though it was difficult. His heart was beating so fast it almost hurt, and he could feel sweat beginning to form on his forehead and palms. The sight of the Shadows, even at flight at this great distance, struck terror in him as he had not felt since the night of the attack on the wall. These last weeks the raid on Darrhyn had been an afterthought, something he considered at a remove from himself, as though it had occurred in another lifetime to another person. Now, faced with the creatures, and the reality that soon he would be doing battle with them, panic threatened to overwhelm him. He forced himself to breathe.

He could feel Yuluir looking at him. "How many do you count?" Masiph said, not taking his eyes from the valley.

"A dozen or so," Yuluir said. "Do we pursue, Husem?"

Masiph turned to the suliher. "Remember our duty. No. Besides, they may be trying to draw us into an ambush in the valley. Let the others know what you have seen and send the carrier to me."

Yuluir nodded. "Yes, Husem," he said, and trotted away, signaling to the others with the call of the desert lark that Shadows had been spotted. Masiph did not stray from where he stood, returning his gaze to the Shadows in flight, watching them until they disappeared in the far distance. As he turned to descend back down the rise he was met by Juilhran, the carrier, coming toward him, gloved arm outstretched with two pigeons perched upon it.

"Yuluir says the others have given the all-clear signal, Husem," the carrier said.

"Good," Masiph said, extracting one of the narrow scrolls, a thin brush and some ink he had been given by the provision officer before setting out that morning. Pulling the stopper from the ink well, he dipped the brush in and drew a few careful lines and figures on the scroll, using the code he had been given by Vazeir Gheyuth to let him know that Shadow Men had been sighted, but no danger was apparent, as well as the direction they were heading. He waited a moment for the ink to dry before rolling the scroll up and tying it to one of the pigeon's legs.

Juilhran grasped the other in his free hand and set the pigeon with the message free. It darted into the air, circling upward for a moment before heading north and east to where the main force of the army lay. Both men watched the bird until disappeared from sight.

"Come," Masiph said at last, "we should not linger. There may be more lying in wait."

•••

The woman who brought his food would not look Vyissan in the eye, and was careful not to touch anything as she set the plate on the table. Word had spread among all the servants Vazeir Gheyuth had provided for him then, as it had among all the Renians. They knew what he was. He watched her go, and saw her make a surreptitious warding sign as she crossed the threshold of his tent, exhaling the breath she had held in as well. This had been the nature of his interactions with almost everyone since the march for Esyln had begun three days before. He had always been an outsider and had considered himself used to minor sleights and exclusions, but this proved trying even for him. He had never been a pariah before.

The most trying had been the frosty reception he had received from Vazeir Gheyuth. The Ad Eselte and the Imperial Vazeir had shown an abundance of caution in their dealings with him, but they had betrayed no animus toward him. He was simply the Qraul's emissary, and if he happened to also be an alkemyst, it was of no particular concern. Gheyuth was another matter.

He had made it abundantly clear that he disliked having Vyissan traveling with his army and suspected him of ulterior motives. Guards were assigned to him at all times while they were on the march or at camp—two were posted outside his tent now, ostensibly to provide protection from those among the sulihers who strongly believed in the prohibitions against alkemya. The reality, Vyissan suspected, was that Gheyuth wanted him watched at all times.

It would all have been at least somewhat bearable if he had someone to talk with. Even imprisoned in the palace there had been Het and the Vazeir, however reticent. He found himself feeling oppressed and nervous without cause while in his tent or at march with the army, his only solace in the evenings, once they had made camp and air had cooled enough that he could wander with ease. Then he would go to the edge of camp and beyond to where the sentries lay scanning the horizon for signs of the Shadows, where he would sit and watch the sun as it descended, lighting the sky afire with red, purple and yellow. Sometimes he would stay until the sun had disappeared entirely, darkness taking hold, Senteur's stars populating the vast sky, and he would stare at them in awe.

He did the same after he finished his meal. By then the heat had gone from the day and a breeze was stirring, cooling the sweat from his brow. He traced the same path he had the other nights, moving among the various quadras encamped around him, yet staying apart, making his way to the rear of the camp, where the sutlers had their tents and their wares. He kept an eye out for the follower he had seen the other night, the one with Shadow Men blood to her shade, but he did not see her among the women out washing pots and robes. From there he passed to where the bawling ardeh were kept, some still yoked to their wagons, and past that to where the latrines had been dug, and beyond to where the first line of sentries had been set.

He stood watching the sunset, enjoying the breeze upon his face, the sky a glorious cascade of colors descending in the distance on the horizon that never seemed quite to vanish. This was an infinite realm, a realm of possibilities. He thought of the woman again, part Shadow, part Renian, and wondered how she had come to be here. There were only a handful of Shadow Men slaves among the army's servants, no doubt because of the fear they would betray their masters at some point. He was used to that fear, had felt it daily from many of the Council, even after he had been made Disciple of the High Adept.

The rustling of the scrub alerted him to the approach of his guards. They followed him everywhere, of course, always maintaining a discreet distance, but leaving him to his own devices. He turned to see what they wanted and saw that Vazeir Gheyuth was with them. Vyissan bowed to the man. "How can I help you, Husem?"

The Vazeir grimaced at his words. "What are you doing out here?"

"Taking the air," Vyissan said, gesturing at the sunset. "Is there a problem, Husem?"

"You tell me. You come here each night and wait until darkness falls. What for, exactly?"

"As I said, I like to take some air before bed. I like to watch the sunset." Vyissan said, careful to conceal his thoughts. What did they suspect him of doing?

"You cannot do that from the fire like the rest of the men?" Gheyuth said, thrusting his face into Vyissan's. "You may have fooled Ibrazol and the Ad Eselte with your charlatanry, but you will not seduce me with your magicks. I know better than to trust an Enir who is willing to forsake all that is sacred to our ancestors. If you are consorting with the Shadow Men out here, if this is some trap that you have lured us into, we will find out."

Vyissan forced himself to remain calm in the face of the Vazeir's aggression, though he could feel the color rising on his face. "Do you think a Shadow could conjure the seal of the Qraul of Craitol, Husem? Whatever you may think of us, we share the same hatred and fear of the Shadows you do. Why else would we propose an alliance and give so much to ensure you would join with us?"

"Then you will have no fear of being watched," Gheyuth said.

"I have made no protest thus far," Vyissan said, gesturing to the two guards who stood stone-faced behind the Vazeir.

Gheyuth glanced at them and smiled. "Well, they will be watching, and we will see if you are telling the truth. See that you remain within camp at all times; your actions could provoke suspicions among my men, and I cannot promise they will be as restrained in their dealings with you as I have been."

"Your discretion credits you, Husem," Vyissan said, and followed the Vazeir as he stalked back toward the camp. The guards allowed him to pass between them before following a step behind until he had returned to his tent, where they resumed their sentinel's watch of his virtue.

10

Donier chewed the lukewarm gruel the woman had given him, wincing at its taste, the sludge sticking to his teeth and seeming to draw all the moisture from his mouth. He set his bowl on the ground and gulped some water.

"It can't be that bad," Ludenn said as he sat beside him, stretching his legs out so they were near the fire.

"We will be lucky to reach Esyln alive," Donier said.

Ludenn laughed. "I will have a talk with our procurer. What was his name?"

Donier shrugged, looking as half the cohort trickled in and settled themselves around the fire. The others were at another fire where the new second, Inagryl, was keeping them company.

"Best to call him the ravager," one of the men said as he sat down across from Donier. "Our guts will all be ravaged tomorrow."

Ludenn took a tentative mouthful and made a face. "I will speak with the man tonight."

Donier forced himself to eat the rest of his bowl, though it became more repulsive the more he ate. The days to come would only grow more difficult, as they began full-day marches through the desert. There would be skirmishes with the Shadow Men, as well as the heat, the wind and the sun. It would all take its toll. Some would not make it to Esyln, he knew, and he wanted to be sure he was not among them.

To this point their pace had been slow, as they waited for the stragglers among the Gvers whose cohorts had not yet rendezvoused with the Qraul's force. The Lastl cohorts had set out from that city two days before heading south and east along the old imperial highway until they reached the Buihel Pyrsedy, one of the watchtowers that marked the border between the desert and Craitol. The Qraul's forces, including the Enir mercenaries, were already camped there, along with the Takyl cohorts and those of a few other Gvers. The peninsular cohorts had begun arriving late in the afternoon—Donier could see them now setting up their camps—and the rest of Gvers and their cohorts were expected by late morning.

They would not be here to see them arrive. The Lastl and Takyl cohorts were to set out at first light, as they knew the territory, setting the pace for the invasion. The rest of the army, barring any issues, would catch up in the days to follow. According to the men on watch at the pyrsedy there had been no sign of the Shadows for days, so Donier did not expect they would encounter any trouble. One could never tell with the Shadow Men, though; they moved like the wind, appearing where least expected.

Ludenn excused himself from the fire, saying he was going to speak with the sutler about his provisions, though Donier knew he was retreating to his tent, where the woman he had brought for the journey awaited him. That was the luxury a man of the second rank could afford. Donier had been tempted to do the same with his reward coins, though in the end he had resisted. If Ulrien had been willing to come with him, it would have been another matter. Instead, he had spent a little coin to ensure he had his own tent and would not be sleeping with the rest of the cohort, and with the rest he would see if there was a woman here worth spending it on. If their food was anything to go by, he thought it unlikely.

Slowly he became aware that everyone around the fire had turned their attention to him, and he drew away from his thoughts and looked at the men.

"Do you believe this nonsense about the Shadows having the engines, Nes Donier?" one of the men asked.

"This is what the High Adept claimed at the Council. The Gvers believed it truth."

"They would do what he said regardless. They are his coins for stamping."

Donier shrugged, refusing to be drawn into their debate. It

would not do for a man of rank to be caught belittling others, even an Adept, with their lessers.

"You should take care not to let your thoughts wander, Nes Donier," a man called Becir said. "Who knows what is lurking in the shadows of the desert. A moment's inattention and who knows what might befall you."

There was something in how he said it that gave Donier pause, the barest hint of menace underlying the jesting tone.

Donier eyed the man, trying to recall what he knew of him, and realized there was little that he did. He decided to take the comment in jest, and said, "There are Shadows in the shadows. We all know what will happen to them."

There were murmurs of half-agreement from the others around the fire. Little excitement had been engendered by the invasion of the desert among the common soldiers. Donier sympathized with them, for it would be a difficult journey across an unrelenting landscape, with little reward likely at the end. The Shadow Men had no cities and palaces to plunder.

"Strange things can happen in the desert," Becir said, and an uncomfortable silence settled across the men.

Was the man threatening him, Donier wondered? An agent of the Veil, perhaps, though he didn't think they would bother with vague threats if they wanted him murdered. And he couldn't see why they would; he was valuable to them alive.

"Yes, I too have eaten this stew," he said, and everyone laughed, including Becir.

The moment seemed to pass, and the conversation carried on to other matters and Donier thought no more of it. Later, though, he caught Becir staring at him, and when he got up to retire to his tent for the evening, he noticed the man was still watching him. As he left the gleam of the fire, disappearing into the darkness, Donier was certain he could feel Becir's eyes upon him, and that indeed was strange and, he thought, would bear watching.

•••

"We should have insisted he come," Laterala was saying as he took another heavy drink of wine. "The other Gvers have all come. Why not him? It makes me look weak."

No, the fact that you do the bidding of the High Adept makes you look

48

weak, Keleprai thought, but did not say. That Cepedutherupt slept in the same tent as the young Qraul, no matter how vast and multi-compartmented it might be, put too fine a point on his servitude. The boy was oblivious to such concerns, though, never worrying about how he would appear to the Gvers.

Keleprai had seen the world as boy did, but now he understood that he was not a ruler but a servant to another's base desires. A realm in which the Council controlled all alkemya was a realm the High Adept ruled. No matter the pieties and abstractions he might spout in speeches and in his conversations, there was the truth of the matter laid plain. Everyone could see it except for the boy.

"The others are not here because you bid them to be, but because they think they can gain your favor by being here," Keleprai said, replenishing both their cups. "This is not their war. This is the High Adept's war. And they have been promised things and they want to see what more is to be gained."

"They should be here because I have commanded them. I am the Qraul," Laterala said. "Perhaps after we triumph they will come to my bidding as they should."

"Perhaps," Keleprai said. "But I doubt it. All realms desire balance, and yours is no different, whatever the rituals might say. The Great Families will always struggle against what the Qraul seeks to impose, just as the families of Lastl struggle against me. It is enough that all the Gvers are represented here, if not present."

Laterala silently mulled this thought, and Keleprai resisted a sigh. He was frightened about what might happen when the boy first tasted the chaos and blood of battle. He would insist on being at the center of things, leading the forces as his father had in Kragi, when that was the last place he should be. Perhaps Cepedutherupt would work his conjuring on him and convince him otherwise, but Keleprai doubted it. The wound of the Gvers doing as they pleased without regard for his office would only continue to fester, and he would think, not without cause, that the only way to prove his worth to them was in the flames of battle.

One of the women Laterala had brought with him drifted into the room and said, "I wish to lie down, Most Gracious. The heat is so bothersome."

"Of course," Laterala said, rising from his seat and moving to help her within, to the room where his bed was. She was a northern trull, with their dark hair that turned auburn in the sun and the narrow, slanting eyes. Too fine-boned for Keleprai's tastes, but since the Qraulla had begun to assert herself, the boy had sought other women in her image. A strange desire. But he had always been too easily swayed by whichever wind happened to be blowing.

The High Adept slipped into the room so quietly that Keleprai was startled from his thoughts, nearly spilling his cup.

"Apologies," Cepedutherupt said as he sat down across from him, glancing around to see where Laterala was. Keleprai jerked his head to the room where the Qraul had disappeared, and from where he could hear soft whispers emanating.

Cepedutherupt nodded and leaned forward, motioning for Keleprai to do the same, and whispered, "We may have an issue with the Renians." Keleprai nodded. "Vyissan has informed me that the Vazeir who is leading their forces does not trust him."

Keleprai shrugged. "What can we do? We cannot turn around now; we have set on this path."

Cepedutherupt pushed a hand through his hair, looking very haggard suddenly. "Nothing. There is nothing we can do. We must strike at the Shadows now while there is still time. But if the Renians turn against us. If they refuse to honor our alliance, we will fail."

"To say nothing of what will happen with the Desu if there promised silk trade vanishes."

Cepedutherupt waved a hand. "That is a passing concern."

Keleprai looked at the High Adept, unable to disguise his shock. "How so? If we are forced to renege on our agreement with the Desu, they will return to the Apysel's arms. We will need their coins after this adventure or we could lose the entire Realm."

"They can be placated," Cepedutherupt said, seeming distracted by other thoughts. "They can be placated. The greater concern is the spread of the engines. If the Shadows are able to escape, all realms will be under threat."

Keleprai felt the bile rising in his throat. They were risking everything to chase the Shadows in the desert, and the High Adept did not care. If they all perished out here but the Shadow Men were vanquished and the knowledge of alkemya remained with the Council, he would count it a victory, no matter that the Apysel would rule Craitol. Because it didn't matter who was Qraul or which of the Great Families were ascendant—the Council Adepts would still hold the balance of power. They were the true Qrauls of the Realm.

The whispers from within the Qraul's bedchamber had stopped, but now they were replaced by another sound, the volume steadily increasing. Cepedutherupt shook his head. "He does not lack for ardor."

"No, pity his broth has no meat to it."

"He is young yet," the High Adept said with a shrug.

"If the young Qraulla is clever, and I think she is, she will be supping on a banquet while her husband is afield. Someone will have potency to unleash her bounty, and when we return your Qraul will have his heir."

Cepedutherupt frowned, hesitating before choosing to say nothing. He was uncomfortable with such talk, but he had always been something of an ascetic. Strange in an Adept, all of whom were notorious for using their conjuring to seduce ladies of the court. Tehh had been legendary in his younger days. Keleprai was surprised that the High Adept had not attempted to instill some of his spirit in Alieren and grant himself an heir. No doubt he would consider such things beneath his domain.

"So you fear the Renians will abandon us to the Shadows and deprive you of your Disciple," Keleprai said, turning the conversation back to more comfortable ground for the High Adept.

He nodded, pushing a hand through his hair again. He was showing his age at last, Keleprai thought, studying him, the weight of all his machinations coming to bear now that the matter was at hand. "But you are right. There is nothing to be done but hope that Vyissan can keep them to the task. Gods grant it so."

"What if he cannot?" Keleprai said. "What if, Gods forbid, the Renians decide to form an alliance with the Shadows?"

"Then all realms are at an end, for the balance can never be restored." The High Adept stood. "I must give blood to Melinon."

Keleprai nodded, raising his cup of wine, and was left alone to listen to the Qraul's exertions through the canvas. *The poor boy*, he thought, *does not know it will all be for naught.*

11

Phariayh sat where the Enir had gestured for her to, watching him from the corner of her eye, being sure to keep her gaze downcast so that he could not see the excitement she felt at being there with him in the splendor of his tent. He was watching her too, as he poured wine into a cup worth almost as much as Fush had paid for her in the market. She knew who he was now; the whole camp was afire with talk of him. He was the Qraul's emissary from Craitol, and an Adept. Atasem was his name.

There were guards with him everywhere, for it was said the Vazeir feared the Craitolians were in league with the Shadows, and that this invasion was a ruse to draw the imperial army into the desert where it could be destroyed, leaving Renuih open for conquest. Many of the men in the cuadras, especially those who grumbled about the conditions of their journey through the desert, believed it to be true. One could not trust an alkemyst after all. The women who had served him said that you could not touch anything in his tent, for he had charms laid everywhere that could ensnare the unsuspecting.

Phariayh had no qualms about that. Let him charm her, let her become ensnared. Better that than another night submitting herself to Fush.

Atasem sat across from her, sipping at his wine, and she allowed herself to meet his gaze. "Thank you for seeing me," he said, as though the choice had been hers. This was the way of the Nohritai, though: thanking you for acceding to their commands, when refusal would mean punishment.

She did not reply, waiting for him to reveal his intentions. She had assumed he would want a warm body at his side for the night—that, after all, was why all the followers were invited to the tents of the sulihers. But surely an emissary of the Qraul could afford a finer quality of woman than she. Surely he could have used his charms to conjure any woman in Darrhyn to follow him into the desert. Which meant he might have other interests in her. Did he require a familiar? She would abase herself before her ancestors if it meant escaping from Fush. They would not blame her.

He paused and swallowed, and Phariayh allowed herself to steal a glance at him. The Adept appeared, if such a thing were possible, to be nervous and unsure of himself. She gave him a flash of a smile, hoping that would help him find the courage for whatever he was about to say.

He smiled reflexively in turn and at last found his words, saying, "I am wondering about your origins. Your shade is quite unique. How did you come to be in this army?"

"My father was a Shadow," she said, knowing what he wanted to hear.

"I see," Atasem said with a nod, his face pinched as though in concern for her. "And how did he come...to know your mother?"

"Their congress, you mean?" Phariayh said, and received a hurried nod from the Adept.

She immediately felt more at ease, even as Atasem's discomfort was evident. She knew his kind. There were those multitudes, like the sulihers and her fellow camp followers and Fush, who were disgusted and repelled by what she represented, the joining of a Renian and a Shadow. Atasem was the opposite side of that same coin, where the revulsion and fear were transmuted somehow into desire and fascination for that unholy object.

Her old master, the one who had purchased her debt from the sanctuary, had been such a man. He had despised and desired her in equal measure, lying with her and then beating her for having the blood of the demons that had so possessed him. His wife had seen through the thin veil of his excuses and had eventually tired of her husband's nighttime sorties to the servant's quarters, which he did little to hide from any of his family, and insisted that he sell Phariayh.

A slaver had purchased her, thinking to turn an easy profit with a properly trained woman, only to discover she was with child. He had forced her to take some concoction prepared by a Healer, which had caused her to fall into a fever and vomit and bleed for days. By the time she had recovered, the war had been upon them and the slaver had been able to turn a tidy profit with the desperate Fush. And so she had come to be here.

She said none of this to Atasem the Adept of Craitol. "I do not know," she said, and saw the flicker of disappointment pass across his face. "I was abandoned to a sanctuary. They raised me and taught me my trade, and when I came of age they sold me to the first family that would take me."

"And when was that?"

"Eight months ago."

"And how did you come to be here? There were no houses that would take you?"

Phariayh shook her head. "No," she said, preferring not to tell him about her old master. It was hard enough to deal with the memories that came, let alone to talk about it with a stranger.

"It must have been a difficult time," he said, smiling at her as though to say that he understood. How could the emissary of the Qraul understand such things?

Phariayh shrugged. "It is the life my ancestors have granted me."

"We all have our burdens," the emissary said. "None of us is our own master."

"You are," she said. "You are an emissary of the Qraul." She said the words as though she could imagine no more exalted a position. And, in truth, she could not. What difference was there to her between the Ad Eselte, the High Nohritai and this man? They all looked upon people like her as ardehs to be yoked, no matter the kindness they might effect.

Atasem laughed, his face wrenched into a bitter smile. "I am a prisoner here. I was a prisoner in Darrhyn. The only reason I am here is because I do the bidding of others."

Phariayh allowed herself to meet his eyes, feeling the thrill of her daring course through her. They were darker eyes than most Enir, and she wondered if that was because of his being a conjurer. His expression and his gestures were without violence, almost tender, so unlike the men she had known, like Fush, who sought to assert their possession of her with every gesture and deed.

"But you are an Adept," she said. "You can bend all men to your will. Surely you can magick yourself from any prison."

He laughed again and shook his head. "No, it is nothing like that, alkemya. Nothing at all. I could destroy a man certainly, though we are forbidden from doing so, except in the most extreme circumstances, but I cannot command his thoughts."

She considered this for a moment and then decided to press her daring further. "Do you desire a familiar? I am unlearned in the arts, but I am tainted by demon blood, as you can see, so I can be of some use, ancestors know. If you offered an honest price for my debts to the sutler, he would certainly take it."

Atasem was startled by her boldness and was rendered momentarily speechless. For a moment Phariayh feared she had gone too far, but he regained himself and laughed, saying, "The art is not like that. We have no familiars."

He paused for a moment, thinking about what he had said, as though just realizing something. "Not exactly familiars, anyway. But I have no need of you in that way. I would not dream of denying you your ancestors' embrace."

Phariayh felt hope, so tantalizing moments ago, drain from her. He was no different than the sulihers, he wanted only a night's comfort, but she would remain Fush's. "I have no ancestors," she said, allowing her feelings to come to forefront.

Seeing her hurt, Atasem reached out to put his hand upon hers. "Even Shadows have ancestors, no matter what others may say. They are men in their way."

"How would you know?"

Atasem considered his words. "There are people in Craitol, northerners, Kragians they are called, as pale as the Shadows are dark. Some call them the Shadows mirrors. But they are men, just like any other, and the Shadows are the same."

Phariayh looked at him, disbelieving, unsure why he was telling her this and what he was trying to say. "Have you met any Shadows?"

"Only you," the emissary said, and squeezed her hand, looking into her eyes. Phariayh knew what was expected of her then, and, stifling her feelings, she set about to comply.

•••

A hand, firm and insistent, upon his shoulder started Masiph awake, and he fumbled with his sheets, struggling to find the dagger he kept on his person as visions of Shadows slitting his throat where he lay invaded his groggy thoughts.

"Lacking your point, are you?" a soft voice said, from somewhere in the darkness. "No wonder you lie alone, Husem."

There was laughter in the voice, which Masiph, fear having blasted any sleep from his mind, now recognized. "I was only trying to find room for you, Yuluir," he said, his voice sounding higher than he wanted. "I assumed you were the trull I had called for."

"Sadly no, Husem," the suliher said. "Your hour is upon you."

Masiph sighed and thanked the suliher, dismissing him as he climbed from bed. He stood for a moment, letting his eyes adjust fully to the darkness, and then dressed, pulling the thin chain mail on over his inner robe, followed by his outer robe. His sword he belted to his side before picking up his spear and shield and proceeding out into the darkness. Boereneth awaited him there, looking half asleep still as he stood at attention, and they made their way beyond the army's encampment to the sentry post, where Nustef and Duhalleh stood on watch.

"Who goes there?" Nustef called out as they approached.

"The alkemyst's familiars," Masiph replied, the password for the evening, one which many of the quadra's had been using, a bitter and uneasy joke.

"Pass forward, Jetthir," Nustef said. Masiph and Boereneth came forward to the post.

"We are here to relieve you."

"We are ready to be relieved," Nustef said, clapping a hand on his shoulder. "Not even the wind is stirring tonight." He passed him a half empty bottle of mehcuil, a drink fermented from cactus leaves. "A gift from our friends in Caijar's quadra to help keep you warm."

"Wonderful," Masiph said, taking a pull on the bottle. It was sweet and bitter in the same instant, and a warm burn went down his throat and spread through his chest. He passed the bottle to Boereneth, and the youth took a pull as well, coughing as he did so.

Masiph glanced at the suliher, a clever word ready, but seeing his miserable expression, made more so by the shadows draped across his face, he held his tongue and instead turned his attention to the vast surrounding darkness. A thousand Shadows could have been hidden there, only a false step possibly betraying their approach as they launched an attack, but Masiph felt no fear. To this point in their march to Esyln they had only seen the backsides of the Shadow Men, sparse tribes fleeing in their wake. Soon enough they would have to stand and fight or risk ceding the whole desert to Renuih, and Masiph looked forward to that day, whenever it might come.

For now he enjoyed the quiet of the night. The sky overhead was gorgeous, stars glimmering, the moon near full and heavy on its descent, and he watched it for a time, lost in its enchantment. How often had he dreamed of such a sky, the heavens of the desert with their strange stars? This was what he had imagined, this moment of perfect stillness, all realms gone quiet, awaiting something. Ancestors had blessed him with this chance, this war, to witness such moments as this.

Beside him Boereneth coughed again, intruding upon Masiph's serenity and drawing him from his contemplation. The silence, which for a moment had seemed absolute, now revealed itself incomplete. Behind them he could hear the odd stirring of those in the camp. Men getting up to go the latrine, or to spell off the sentries, the whispers of those who could not sleep, the sighs of a lovers' embrace, all of them seemed to be present, a hushed cacophony drowned in the vast emptiness of the desert. Masiph felt unsteady on his feet, and took another swig of the mehcuil to regain his equilibrium.

He reached out to pass the bottle to Boereneth, but the suliher waved him away. Masiph turned to look at him and saw that the youth was shivering, his hand shaking so violently that he could barely hold on to his spear and shield.

"Are you ill, Suliher?" Masiph said.

"Just a chill, Husem. I will be fine."

Masiph nodded. "Good. Drink this. It will help."

He passed him the bottle, and Boereneth drank from it deeply, though his shivering did not stop. After a moment he walked away from the sentry post, and Masiph could hear him retching. When he returned, Masiph told him to go and send someone else to man the watch. "You are no good to anyone here, Suliher."

The youth agreed, saying in parting, "There was blood in my shit last night."

Masiph watched Boereneth disappear, swallowed by the darkness, and found himself seized by a chill as well. Blood in the urine or shit, along with the fevers could only mean one thing: the flux. If it had set upon the army, the Shadows would be the least of their worries.

12

There were no Shadows upon the desert, at least none that they had seen, and the cohorts were growing restless, their desire for blood growing stronger even as a lingering unease began to edge into their thoughts the farther into the desert they went. Would they lose themselves in this place, as so many had said before whenever an invasion of the desert had been proposed, whether at court or in a drinkery, chasing Shadows? The kehels and seconds merely repeated what their Gvers, who themselves were beginning to feel anxious about the entire enterprise, had told them: they were marching to the ruined city Esyln there to face the Shadow Men and their alkemysts. And what if they should find only ruins there, the men asked, and to that there was no answer.

The answer, Donier thought as he relieved himself in the latrine dug the night before, was that the Council Adepts would decide the matter, letting the Gvers and the Qraul think the decision was theirs. That was how they had ended up here in the first place, after all. The Adepts would take them everyone to their doom all over a couple of engines.

Donier spat when he was finished and clapped his hands together, a ritual begun sometime in his youth and now done unconsciously, though he could not have told anyone of its providence. He picked his way among the still-slumbering cohorts, going mostly by memory, dawn still a little way off, though there was a hint of light on the horizon. A false light, he knew; the sun would not arise for at least another hour.

He had become used to the desert in the last week, now knew its rituals. There was the false light before morning, the endless sunsets that seemed to color the whole sky, the wind that would pick up late in the morning and die as evening settled in, to say nothing of the unrelenting heat of the day and surprising cool of the night. The vastness of it all, these endless landscapes, red rocked or dull green, fading to brown with scrub, and the scent of sage everywhere.

It was the place of his dreams, he realized. It all had the same feel, the same absence of any other living things, and the silence but for the wind. The valley where he had walked endlessly he felt certain was here somewhere, though he had no urge to discover it and the destination he had been seeking. The Gods, though, would decide the matter, he knew. He could only thank them that the dreams had absented themselves since the march into the desert had begun.

His thoughts were still upon the dreams as he slipped into his tent, hoping to get another hour's sleep before duty called him forth, so he did not notice the other man's presence until the hand was at his throat and the point of the dagger was pressed into his back.

"We have much to discuss, you and I," Becir whispered.

"Do we now?" Donier said, his mouth gone very dry.

"You failed us in Craitol."

The Veil, Donier realized. "I did as you asked," he said, keeping himself still. He needed to piss again, but he tried not to think about that, forcing himself to breath.

"You most certainly did not. What did the man at the Council tell you?"

The dagger shifted slightly, its point digging at his skin. Donier closed his eyes, offering an invocation to Melinon that these terrible moments would not be his last. He thought briefly about trying to overpower Becir, but the grip on his throat was firm—it was very difficult to breathe—and the dagger needed only a little force to find its mark, which the man would be able to achieve before Donier had managed to free himself. He would have to wait and hope the Gods presented himself with a chance.

"He told me to make myself absent for a moment. And I did."

"You returned before the deed was done and stopped the man from the killing the Gver."

Donier swallowed. "It is not my fault he was so slow at his task. I did all that was asked of me. Gave him a moment's absence. The Adept Tehh ordered me to return. I could not disobey him."

"There was still no need to kill the man when you did," Becir said, more loudly than he had intended. He continued in a hushed whisper, "You could have let him finish the job before landing your blow."

It was a good thing they were arguing over deeds past, Donier told himself—it meant they did not intend just to kill outright. He was still useful to them, they just wanted to make sure he understood that his debt to them had not been met. But he had known that already, for it never would.

"The Disciple had him. He was not killing anyone that day."

"So you say," Becir said, though he did not sound as though he believed him or particularly cared. "Your failure cost us dearly that day. But no matter; the coin shall be repaid. We shall do at last what needs to be done and begin a cleansing of this realm."

"You intend to try to kill the Gver again?" Donier said. Even as he spoke, he knew in his heart what the response would be, and felt sick and cold.

"Yes, and you shall do it for us."

"I will not," Donier said, raising his voice above a whisper, though not so loudly it could be heard beyond the tent. A cough from somewhere nearby, a man shifting in his sleep, stilled them both.

The knife left his back and was pressed into his throat, the point lifting his chin up. "You will," Becir said, "or you will die."

"You cannot make me," Donier said, affecting a bravado he did not feel. "I am the second of this cohort. I can have you flogged or worse at a word."

Something like a laugh came from Becir. "Do you think these men follow you and Ludenn? For now you do, but if you start whipping men without cause, how long do you think you will last when the battle starts?"

"A cause can be found. We have stood together in battle before, do not forget. I know their hearts better than you," Donier said, though he wondered if that were in fact true.

"You are a fool," Becir said. "But it is no matter whether or not you have me killed. Do you think I am the only one here amongst the cohorts? There are others who will see that you do your duty."

"What is your plan, then? What would you have me do?"

Becir laughed again. "I am no fool, Nes Donier. When the time comes, we will speak again."

The knife and hand were withdrawn from his throat, and Becir vanished outside without stirring the tent. Donier forced a ragged breath into his lungs and sat down on his bed, pressing his hands between his knees to stop them from shaking. He remained where he was as the sun crept into the sky, watching the light fill the tent, until the horns called the cohorts to rise for the day.

13

It was the quadra led by Ibrazol's son where the first signs of flux appeared, which should have been no surprise to Gheyuth. The boy was ill-starred and always had been. He should never have been elevated, and if it had not been for his father, who had spent all these years trying to make something of that feeble stock, the Vazeir of the Imperial Army would have made certain the boy remained in Darrhyn. As it was, he was here and so now was the cursed flux. Nothing bled an army like a plague, and flux itself was particularly insidious, leaving men dried-out husks, racked by fevers, and unable to keep any food or water in them.

There had been men in Masiph's quadra who showed signs of the sickness yesterday morning, and before camp had broken, a half-dozen more had been found throughout the rest of army. By nightfall that number had increased to twenty, thirty if one counted the slaves, and now this morning the Chief Healer had arrived before dawn to say that another thirty had entered the first stages of the plague. The situation threatened now to spiral beyond all control, and here they were five days' march from the borders of the Empire in the middle of an unfamiliar and forbidding desert. By ancestors' grace they had not encountered any Shadows, though that might change now.

"How grave is the situation?" Chisin said to the Healer, in a tone that demanded that the correct answer, whatever it might be, be given. The Hjai was a brute of a man, looming over everyone menacingly, with a square head that seemed carved from the desert rock. An utterly intimidating presence, yet despite appearances he had a surprisingly subtle mind, both qualities that the Vazeir valued in his second.

The Healer blinked but otherwise showed no signs of quailing before the Hjai, which Gheyuth took as a good sign. The man would not crumble in a difficult situation.

"Very grave, Husem," the Healer said, looking from the Vazeir to the Hjai. "Of those who have fallen ill already, I do not expect many to live past the day, ancestors forbid. If we do not halt, the flux will continue to spread. It is a pernicious disease. It could overwhelm the entire force."

Gheyuth put a hand to his temple. He could feel the beginnings of a headache forming behind his thoughts. There had just been an endless series of problems since they had begun their march, in part because of the hurried nature of preparations, which had left them under-provisioned and scrambling for weapons and ardeh, among other things. If the Ad Eselte or the Imperial Vazeir had seen fit to include him in their discussions with the Qraul's emissary, matters might have been different, but they had not.

The emissary was another matter altogether. Gheyuth did not trust the man, though he had at least ceased his nightly migrations into the desert. But he was an Adept, so that did not mean he could not be communicating with the Shadows through other alkemycal means. After all, he claimed to be in communication with the Qraul at all times. Gheyuth suppressed a shudder. That an Enir could so forsake his ancestors did not bear thought. That the Ad Eselte could join the Empire in league with such a man, no matter what promises he might make, well—perhaps Osiphan had not been so wrong about the man. He was a philosopher, given to logic and reason, but sometimes men could be led by logic to a place beyond reason, which was where Gheyuth found himself now, trapped in the desert with an army succumbing to the flux, exposed to the Shadow Men with an ancestors-forsaken alkemyst in their midst.

He became aware that both Chisin and the Healer were waiting for him to speak, his thoughts having taken him away from the matter at hand. He looked to the Healer. "And halting will stop the spread?"

"If we establish a quarantine of those infected, yes, Husem," the Healer said. "That is the only way."

"A quarantine? A separate camp?"

"Yes. I will need volunteers to assist in the care of the sick as well."

"You will have them," Gheyuth said. "Your thoughts?" he asked Chisin.

"We cannot halt the march here. There is no water, and the ground is not good to defend. If we must establish a more permanent camp—two camps with the quarantine—we shall want to make sure we can hold the ground easily. The Shadows will surely try their luck with a raid if we are not on the move."

Gheyuth nodded. "Agreed. How far to better ground and water?"

Chisin motioned with his hand, and a courtier brought forward a small table, which he set out between them, while another rolled out a map.

"Here," Chisin said, placing a thick finger in the middle of the map, "is Uigahel. It should be a day's march south from here, more or less. It was a watering stop on the old road. According to the imperial records, the river flowed most years throughout the rains. Perhaps some of the old town is left and we can use it for defenses."

"There is nothing on the highway?" Gheyuth said.

"Two days at least. There is an old water stop on the highway where we were planning to camp tonight, but it is just a spring. It may not be flowing now, and we may overwhelm it if we have to stay there for longer than a night. The best water is at Uigahel if we are going to be stopping for some time. Otherwise..." Chisin shrugged.

"How many days will we need to keep the quarantine?" Gheyuth said, turning back to the Healer.

He shrugged in turn. "I couldn't say. The flux will need to run its course. Sometimes that is a day or two, but this, I think, will be worse. The men are grievously ill, and it has spread so quickly."

Gheyuth considered this for a moment, tapping his finger at his temple, staring at the map as though to will another solution from its scratchings. Finally he waved it away and stood. "Let the jetthirs know that we make for Uigahel and we will establish camp and quarantine there until the flux has passed," he said to Chisin. "Ancestors grant the Shadows do not find us there. Let the quadras know we will need volunteers to see to the ill."

He paused for a moment, looking from face to face. "Let us hope the men are made of stern stuff, or we may have other problems to deal with soon enough."

He did not need to elaborate; both the Healer and Chisin would know what he meant. Mutiny. The thought filled him with dread. How many imperial armies had been torn apart by a quadra or two, fearful of the flux or whatever other superstitious nonsense they gave credence to, rising up or deserting and forcing the rest of their fellows to put them to the sword? They could ill afford even the most minor of uprisings here in the desert, where things could quickly spiral beyond control and where no other imperial forces could be sent to reinforce them.

"You are dismissed, gentleman," Gheyuth, forcing himself not to dwell on such thoughts. If the time came, he would deal with it then. "We march in an hour."

As the two men left his tent, a thought occurred to him, and he grimaced and called for one of his courtiers. "Bring me that cursed emissary. He will need to know of our change in plans."

•••

Little remained of Uigahel, as the Renians called it, a former imperial town of little consequence nestled in the curve of a thin river. The walls of the town were still in place here and there, though what was left was crumbling, and the small fortress where the imperial soldiers had been garrisoned was largely intact. It would serve well enough to provide a base while the flux ran its course, the fortress providing a perfect quarantine for the diseased. The quadras were busy establishing sentry posts and adding to the meager defenses offered by the town walls, dragging wind-worn stone from other long-abandoned buildings to reinforce what was there. Others were busy in the fortress setting up beds for the flux-ridden, and tending to those in their last hours.

Vyissan had offered to assist in this efforts—he had some skill in thaumaturgy after all, though he was wise enough to make no mention of it—but the Vazeir had refused his offer. "The men will already be looking for someone or something to blame for this plague befalling us, and many will turn to you, especially when the men you are tending to die, as they will," Gheyuth said in a tone that suggested that he believed they would be right to suspect

Vyissan of malfeasance.

The Disciple had offered no argument, just as he had offered no argument when the Vazeir had told him they would be making an encampment and journeying away from Esyln to do so, recognizing it would be futile. Any attempt to argue or dissuade the Vazeir would only be seen as proof of whatever ulterior motive Gheyuth believed resided in his heart. Better to let it lie. Vyissan had not yet told Cepedutherupt of this latest development. There had been enough comments, veiled or otherwise, from Gheyuth, to say nothing of the reactions of the soldiers, that he wanted to wait until he was certain he was alone to send word to the High Adept.

Growing restless at his enforced idleness, Vyissan walked down to the river, though the thin trickling stream he found there hardly seemed to warrant that name. Its banks were high, however, and he recalled the other dry bed he had almost been trapped on during his earlier desert crossing, a stream swollen by a flash of a storm. The river bottom was mostly sand, and he left soft imprints as he walked up to the water. He crouched over it, filling his canteen with care before splashing water on his face and neck.

He stayed kneeling where he was, letting the moisture cool him, thinking about how he would explain what had happened to Cepedutherupt. The High Adept would expect him to act, to try to force the Vazeir to keep the army marching. Every day lost here was another where the Shadows at Esyln could move their engines to another site or plan a counterattack. So long as the two forces were separate they were at risk, especially the Renian Army with no Adepts to counter the Shadow Men engines. Cepedutherupt was right, Vyissan knew: it was essential the two armies rendezvous as soon as possible, before the Shadows had time to organize, but he also knew that no argument he could make would convince Gheyuth of these facts. His very presence here hindered his cause.

A shout roused him from his thoughts, and he stood from the water, turning to see who was calling him. A Nohritai youth, jetthir of his quadra by his robes, was glaring at him with a flushed face from atop the riverbank near one of the crumbling wall remnants his men were reinforcing. Sighing, Vyissan wandered over to the jetthir, keeping his face placid and unconcerned. "How can I help you, Husem?" he said as he approached.

"What are you doing, emissary?" the jetthir said, glancing over his shoulder at his men, who continued working, though a few were watching the confrontation. Vyissan was unsure if the Nohritai wanted his men to see what he was doing, and he seemed unsure himself, hesitating after his blunt question.

"I was getting some water," Vyissan said, gesturing to his canteen. He gave the Nohritai what he hoped was a reassuring smile. It did not have the intended effect. The man seemed to bristle at the sight of it.

"There is water in the camp. I suggest you use it. Others can collect the water."

"It was no trouble. I needed to stretch my legs."

"Are you trying to poison our water as well as giving us the flux?"

The others in the quadra were looking now. Vyissan tried to stay calm, to keep his voice even. This was a dangerous moment now, he could tell. He was on precipice of violence. "Why would I poison the water? I have to drink it as well, don't I? And I could get the flux just as easily as any of you."

"We all know your magicks will protect you."

"Alkemya does not work in that manner."

The youth sneered. "We all know you survived the poisoning by the traitors. Any normal man would have perished."

Vyissan felt himself go cold at those words. How did the jetthir know about that? He could feel the situation moving beyond his control by the second. The others in the quadra had stopped working, and a few had started to move toward the two of them. All of them were grinning, their expressions ugly, without mirth.

Vyissan knew how confrontations like this ended. He had been trapped in situations like these his entire life, whether on the streets of Devew or in the halls of the Council of Adepts, surrounded by Craitolian youths cursing him and his kind for their betrayal of the Realm and art. Once he had been beaten so badly he had been left to die in the street. A thaumaturge had saved him and set him on the path to the Council and Discipledom, which had taken him to the desert and this confrontation, an echo of the past reaching out. The Gods never let you escape, he knew, and they enjoyed the circular paths a life might take back to a journey's beginning.

"That still does not explain why I would poison you, or bring the flux upon you. I am an emissary of the Qraul. I represent him in all things, and he has made alliance with your Ad Eselte." He tried to smile again, but his lips would not cooperate. His mouth was dry, and he looked from suliher to suliher, their faces dark with anger and mistrust.

"Words," the jetthir said, spitting at his feet. "Words. Nothing more. Deeds are what I look at. What a man does."

"I have done nothing. Husem Gheyuth..." Vyissan began to say, raising a placating hand.

"Do you think no one has seen you consorting with the beast? Why she is even here, I can't imagine. That sutler should be strung up for his treason."

The color drained from Vyissan's face, fury pulsing in his blood. *She is no beast*, he wanted to say, to defend Phariayh, but he knew he could not. The jetthir and his sulihers were looking for a reason to attack him, and that would give it to them. What he needed, he thought ruefully, were the charms they thought he possessed to escape this situation.

"Husem Gheyuth has asked me not to be involved in the care for those with the flux or in the preparation for your defenses," he tried again, ignoring the youth's last words. "For some reason he thinks I would be a distraction."

He could not resist this last jab, though he knew it might pay for it grievously, and was rewarded with a mocking smile from the jetthir. The Nohritai looked as though he were about to say or do something more, and Vyissan could feel his own anger building to the point where he wanted him to, wanted to be done with these words and to strike at this pompous young fool. If he could bloody the jetthir's face a bit, it would be worth whatever bruises and indignity he would suffer.

He was saved from himself by the appearance, as if from Senteur's heavens, of the Vazeir's hulking Hjai, who emerged from behind the wall to glare at the sulihers and their jetthirs, who all suddenly found themselves staring at the ground or into the far distance, as though they were busy with some obscure and esoteric contemplation unrelated to whatever else was going on around them.

The Hjai looked from face to face, the silence growing more awkward by the moment. "Sulihers," he said at last, his voice mild and reasonable, "the wall will not rebuild itself."

The men sprang into action, relief washing over their faces, to be given this duty instead of the punishment they had expected. The jetthir did not move, waiting for the Hjai to address him.

"And you, Husem," the Hjai said, putting a mocking emphasis on the honorific, "what exactly do you think you are doing?" There was a long pause in which the Hjai waited for the jetthir to respond. Vyissan saw him swallow and keep his gaze firmly downcast.

"What would your father say if he knew you were threatening the emissary he negotiated an alliance with? There are some here who think you are only here because of your father's name. I would take care that you do not confirm their worst suspicions of your ability."

The Hjai's voice was pitched so that only the jetthir and Vyissan could hear what he said—a small mercy, the Disciple supposed, though the sulihers would have a good idea of what was being said, he was sure. The jetthir at last managed a nod and a mumbled, "Thank you, Husem."

The Hjai dismissed him with a flick of his wrist, and the jetthir turned back to his men, the air seeming to go out of him as he did. "If you would be so kind, emissary," the Hjai said, gesturing for Vyissan to follow him back into the camp. It was not a request, he knew.

They walked back in silence, during which Vyissan realized the significance of what the Hjai had said to the jetthir. That was the Imperial Vazeir's son, the last of his four, the one who had killed his mother in birth. The only one remaining now. He tried to recall what Hasen had told him of the youth. There had been nothing good: he was the youngest son, the forgotten one, marked by a painful memory, and certain not to inherit. Now he was all the Vazeir had, and he had been sent off to battle in this war. Vyissan understood why the youth had confronted him, nearly inciting a brawl over nothing. With the anger against the Qraul's emissary growing among the ranks, he must have feared being tied too closely to the Enir alkemyst just by dint of his lineage.

"A troubling incident," the Hjai said to him. "It will not be the last. The men mistrust you as it is; the flux will only make matters worse. And the Shadows lurk out there somewhere."

"I shall take more care," Vyissan said. "I do not want to be cause of any problems for you or the Vazeir."

"I think it would be wise for you to remain in your tent for the next few days while all this passes. That way we can ensure that you are protected should things go wrong."

Vyissan nodded, knowing that this too was not a request and that he had been, for all intents and purposes, imprisoned.

•••

It took three attempts for Nustef to get to his feet and what felt like half an hour to make his unsteady way to the latrines. A coughing fit halfway there nearly thwarted his efforts, leaving him breathless and lightheaded, but he managed to persevere, and it was with a sense of triumph that he shifted his robes and squatted over the trench to relieve himself. The trip back nearly undid him; for a brief moment he feared he would collapse on the ground and have to be carried back to his bed, but the wave of nausea and dizziness passed and he was able to shuffle his way back through the rows of cots to his own, where he drifted to sleep as soon as he lay down.

When he awoke again, the glare of the sun was in his eyes, the day already hot and dry. A warm breeze stirred the loose bedding among the camp beds that lay row upon row in the Uigahel fortress, carrying the sound of groans and coughs from all the suffering men with it. Nustef kept his eyes closed, feeling exhausted beyond measure and deeply regretting his effort the night before, hoping to stave off the day and its miseries for a few moments longer. It was no use; the noise of the others on their sick beds forced him awake and brought to the forefront of his awareness his own agonies, the ache and fever, the cough that would not subside, and the steady turmoil of his stomach.

He prayed to his ancestors to release him from this suffering; whether he lived or died, he no longer cared. The wind offered no response to his invocations. Perhaps his ancestors had forsaken him, leaving him to wander this terrible plain for all existence, never to reach those that lay beyond. He thought of his family's mausoleum in the Pantheon of the Dead, unattended and in disrepair, home to vagrants or worse, and what little he had done to rectify such a grievous sin. It was no surprise that he had been forsaken. This realm offered little in the way of mercy.

A hand touched his shoulder, and he opened his eyes and saw Masiph crouching over him, an uneasy smile on his face. He cleared his throat. "What are you doing here?"

"I brought some water," Masiph said, holding a canteen, which

Nustef sipped at greedily, realizing how parched he was.

"The quarantine—you should not be here." His own voice sounded strange to Nustef, a hollow echo of his thoughts. He blinked, trying to clear his head.

"I volunteered to be here. There was..." Masiph hesitated, looking off into the distance before deciding not to say what he had been going to. "There are no Shadows nearby. Patrols and sentry duty are boring, and I thought I might be more use here."

"You just wanted to keep a close eye on your bed."

Masiph laughed. "Yes, I don't want it wandering away. At least I know it's in trustworthy hands."

"Don't be so sure," Nustef said, coughing for a moment. "When I am well, I may sell it to the highest bidder."

"If you share the spoils, we may both do well by it. We can each have a woman for the rest of the campaign. Some of the jetthirs are not taking too kindly to sacrificing their luxuries."

"I can imagine. I'll have some more of that water." Masiph helped him drink, and he lay back, enjoying the sensation of the trickle of water descending to his empty stomach. Did he dare eat today, he wondered? Even the broth yesterday had sent him to the latrines.

"How are you feeling?" Masiph said, trying to hide his concern.

"I think the worst is past," Nustef said, managing a smile. He could hear his own labored breathing, which put the lie to his words, and he shrugged. "I'll be up and about soon enough, I expect."

"Of course." Masiph nodded. Again he looked as though he were about to say something but thought better of it. Someone called from across the fortress's courtyard, and he glanced over. "I should go. Let you rest. I'll come back and see how you're doing later today."

"Thank you," Nustef said, glad his friend was gone so that he no longer had to maintain the pretense that all was well.

He closed his eyes again, feeling adrift and without a locus of being, his soul swirling apart. He imagined the wind carrying it beyond the fortress into the desert, where pieces of it were tangled in the sage and scrub to be eaten by tolotes, while others were captured and enslaved by the Shadows. There they remained, toiling for unending days in the desert, the wind his only companion.

14

It had been a tempestuous evening, one which had offered little in the way of sleep, so Keleprai was hardly in the mood to counsel a worried Cepedutherupt before dawn broke. The night had begun well enough, with he and Kigarle sharing far too much wine while playing cards, but took a turn for the worse once he returned to his own tent. The girl he had brought with him on the journey, a dancer he had poached from the Morning's retinue—much to his delight and the Chair's outrage—had been waiting for him, and as soon as he entered the tent she began to attack him, cursing him for a drunken fool and demanding to be returned home to Lastl.

"There is no going back now," he told her, once she had ceased shouting at him. "We are seven days' journey from Lastl."

"I will not stay another day," she said. "There is no one here to talk to."

"You have me to talk to," he said, immediately realizing he had made a grievous error.

"All you do is drink all day with Nes Kigarle or the Qraul. And then you come back here and expect me to stir your cold broth. I am not some trull happy to be the coin you stamp. I was the finest dancer in the Morning. I threw away a fortune for you."

And gained another, he thought but was wise enough not to say. She continued on in that vein for some time, and it was even longer before Keleprai managed to quiet her, babbling promises he had no intention of keeping, so they could retire to bed.

He had only just managed to drift off to sleep when a

tremendous storm erupted above, cataclysmic sounding, with exploding thunder and lightning so bright the night evaporated briefly and it was as day in the tent. This rupture in the heavens was accompanied by howling wind that tore at the cloth of the tent, which mercifully held, though Keleprai could hear that others were not so lucky, as well as torrential rain that sounded like a thousand hammers ringing on a thousand anvils as it struck the ground. Here his fortune did not hold, for the rain soon overwhelmed the tent until it was dripping from a dozen different places while newly formed streams flowed across the ground beneath his camp bed.

There had been no sleeping after that, especially not with the girl complaining bitterly of the damp and the cold that followed in the storm's wake. He had proposed a method of warming her, but that had only sent her into another spiral of complaints about the poor treatment she was receiving and the miserable conditions she was forced to live under while with the army.

"If I had only known," she said again and again, and Keleprai silently agreed. *If only we both had, I might be sleeping even now.*

He had resigned himself to some long hours of silent wakefulness waiting for dawn to come when one of his attendants had come to announce that the High Adept wished to see him. Keleprai had wanted to refuse to see Cepedutherupt, more out of pettiness and frustration than anything else, but the girl had stirred awake at his side and he fled before she could resume her complaints.

"I hope I am not interrupting your sleep," Cepedutherupt said.

Keleprai glanced at the attendant, who was careful to keep his face expressionless. "No matter. What do you wish to discuss?"

Cepedutherupt sat down, giving an exhausted smile. He looked, Keleprai thought, as though he too had not slept at all. "We must stop the march." He repeated what he had said when Keleprai, not believing what he had heard, asked him again.

"Why in the Gods' names must we?"

"I know," the High Adept said with a shake of his head. "I know the risks we face. But we must halt our march. The Renians have encountered some difficulties on their own march and will be delayed. We must coordinate our arrival to Esyln. The Shadows lay in wait there with their engines. If we were to arrive before the Renians…"

His voice trailed off and he looked away. Keleprai swore under his breath. "Have the Shadows attacked them?"

"No," the High Adept said. "Nothing like that. They have hardly seen a Shadow since they entered the desert, just like us. The problem is the old highway. It is in ruins in places, and the going has been tough. They have had to take another route. A longer one. And they are not sure how long it will take them."

Keleprai stared at Cepedutherupt, not believing a word he said. He was lying, or if not lying, at least omitting some of what his Disciple had told him. What was really happening there? He shook his head. "So we are just to wait for them?"

"We have no choice."

"What is a day or two?" Keleprai said. "If we arrive before them, we arrive before them."

"It is everything," Cepedutherupt said, with a vehemence that surprised Keleprai. "My agents with the Shadows have told me what kind of force they possess and how many engines. We cannot stand against them alone. We need the Renians."

"What is to stop them from leaving Esyln and coming against one army or the other? They are watching us, you know. They have been watching us all along."

"Nothing. There is nothing. But I don't think they will," Cepedutherupt said, exhaling softly. "The engines are difficult to move, very difficult. I don't think they will risk it."

"They don't need the engines. If they have enough men, they could overwhelm us regardless."

"Yes," Cepedutherupt said. "Yes, they could."

Keleprai put a hand to his temple. His temptation was to berate the High Adept, to say this had been his worry all along, that wars never unfolded as planned and disaster lay in wait at every turn. It was what he should have said the day of the Council or before, but now it was too late. The disaster was upon them.

"We cannot stay here," he said. "This is no ground to defend. It would be good to find a decent water supply. I do not trust the spring."

"Very well," Cepedutherupt said. "We can march to better ground and water. Where will we find that?"

Keleprai shrugged. "I can't say for sure. The maps we have are old, and I don't know how accurate they are. No one has been this far into the desert in generations."

"Let us consult with the other Gvers, then, and make our best guess. Melinon will guide us."

Keleprai nodded his assent, thinking they would need the guidance of all the Gods to save them now. For the time being, the worry was water and their defense against the Shadows, but soon enough it would be keeping the army fed, for the supplies the sutlers had brought would begin to run out and there was not enough game or vegetation to live on out here. The more he thought about it, the more he realized that they did not need to worry about the Shadows attacking them. If they were cunning, and he had no doubt they were, they would simply wait and let the desert do their work for them.

•••

Two tolotes were calling back and forth from the hills just beyond where the army had set up camp. Probably farther upstream from the trickle of water where they had established their main camp, Donier decided, which meant that if the stories were true and the tolotes were the Shadow Men's familiars, the Shadows were there as well. It was a disturbing thought, given the precariousness of their position, in this river valley surrounded by hills of red-colored rock where nothing seemed to grow.

True, they had lookouts posted on many of the tallest hills where they could see anyone approaching from the surrounding desert and the highway, as well as men stationed along the valley to prevent any unpleasant surprises from that direction. None of that provided much comfort, though, for Donier had no doubt that the Shadows could pass unnoticed through the hills and into the heart of their camp, no matter what precautions they might take. They had seen no one since coming here the day before, just a herd of antelope that had scattered at the sight of them before anyone had time to throw a spear or draw an arrow.

That had been a bitter failure, and had caused much muttering and anger among the cohorts. Donier had been forced to listen to it throughout dinner and breakfast as the men spooned up their thin gruel and fought over the bit of ardeh meat the cohort had been rationed. Rationing was suddenly at the forefront of everyone's thoughts now that the march had been halted for an undetermined amount of time.

Ludenn had gone to a meeting of the kehels with the Gvers

where the halt had first been announced, and had returned shaking his head, saying, "No one will say why. I don't think even they know."

Donier frowned. "Do they understand we are exposed here? That our food is limited?"

"Of course they do," Ludenn said. "Their opinions count for nothing. This is the High Adept's army and we will do as he says, no matter that it may kill us all."

"How long do they expect us to stay here?"

"They do not know," Ludenn said, and Donier swore.

"The men will not be happy."

"No, and why should they be."

They had not been, with the exception of Becir, who saw an opportunity to have Donier carry out his plan for assassinating the Gver while the army was not on the march. It would be easier, he said, to find a cause to be in the Gver's presence while the army was not on the move, though Donier did not see how it made any difference at all. There was no reason for him to be in the Gver's presence at all now. The man had thanked him, paid him his reward, and doubled his personal guard with men that he trusted absolutely, of which Donier was not one. There was almost no chance he could find himself alone with Keleprai, or near enough to him to launch an attack without someone being able to stop him.

Becir would not hear reason, though, and had insisted that Donier arrange the watches so that they would be on duty together, atop a hill away from the others, so that they could go over the plan together. Donier had relented, unable to find an excuse to put the man off. The only saving grace was that he had been able to take the hours just before sunset, when the heat of day began to fade but the light still held. Now he stood, restlessly scanning the horizon and listening to the tolotes' cries, while Becir crouched and worked a quid into his mouth.

"Leave that, there are no Shadows here," Becir said, when he had finished putting the aslyn in his cheek.

"You know as well as I do what the tolotes' howls mean," Donier said, not bothering to turn around.

"Only a woman afraid of her own shadow would pay heed to those tales," Becir said, spitting as he did so. "There are more important matters to deal with now. We need a plan to get you an audience with the Gver."

Donier still refused to turn away from the horizon. "I will not do what you ask of me."

He did not even hear Becir move before the man was behind him, a dagger pressed into his back. "That is not an answer the Veil will accept. Remember, I am not here alone. You will be compelled."

Donier turned his head slightly, catching Becir's eyes from the corner of his own. "You need me alive to do your foul deed. These threats of yours are idle."

"You think so do you," Becir said with a hiss, his lips at Donier's ear. "Your life is forfeit if you do not comply. We can find someone else to kill the Gver if need be."

"Then do it," Donier said with a shrug, "and have done with me."

Becir was silent and very still beside him, and Donier felt the point of the dagger tremble against him. Finally he laughed and said, "You are not so brave. This is not a dice game you can bluff your way out of. Besides, you're a fool if you believe it is only your life that lies in the balance. Your wife, your father, your son. Your family's name. All of it will be left to ruin."

"Very well," Donier said. "What is your plan?"

He was surprised at his calm in the face of such threats, and his knowledge that the Veil would very likely be able to deliver on them. Perhaps it was the distance of the peril here in the desert so far from Lastl, where the Shadows seemed a much more present danger, perhaps it was something about the man himself, but Donier felt no fear of him.

The knife disappeared from his back and Becir squatted, spitting out some more of his quid. He gestured for Donier to join him, which he did, careful to position himself so that he could still see the full sweep of the desert to the highway.

"As I was saying," Becir said. "We need to get you an audience with the Gver. Something where you can get close to him, perhaps even without his guard present."

"The man is no fool," Donier said. "

"He will trust you, after what you did for him at the Council. That is the only good to come out your failure there. We just need a reason."

Donier thought for a moment and smiled bitterly. "Perhaps I

can tell him I have heard rumors of another Veil plot."

Becir laughed. "It is just the thing. Now, they may have you leave your weapons behind when you go into the audience. I have a dagger that can be concealed in the sleeve of your robe. You can bring it to your hand with the flick of a wrist."

"Who will create the distraction?" Becir stared at him, seemingly unsettled by the question.

"I will need a distraction," Donier said, "if I am going to be able to get close enough to the Gver without the guards being able to respond."

"I shall, of course," Becir said with a bravado that made Donier raise his eyebrow.

"You alone will? We need the whole guard drawn away. A mass of confusion, so that I can do the killing without being noticed. Otherwise they will capture me and I will talk. The Adepts will make me. Or were you planning on making your way back through the desert on your own?"

"You can leave it to me," Becir said after a moment. He seemed to be thinking the matter over, as though these eventualities had not occurred to him. "I will arrange with the others to have something done."

"I want to know what the plan is and I want to meet the others. I do not want to leave my life on the line with just anyone."

"Leave it to me," Becir said in a cold voice. "Your life is on the line regardless. Pray to the Gods it does not end before you have the chance to redeem yourself."

Donier nodded and let the matter rest, turning his attention back to the desert, which remained empty as ever. His thoughts were afire with what this last exchange had just told him. Becir was a rank amateur, who had not even given a thought to what might happen if Donier were taken alive. Donier could feel the advantage in the situation turning his way, for the man now realized their fates were tied together.

How many compatriots did he have in the cohorts? Something about the bravado with which he had said that he would handle creating the distraction was telling, Donier thought. Who was the man who had entrapped Becir to this task as he had ensnared Donier? The answer to that question would provide a path forward, he was certain.

15

Phariayh applied the damp cloth to the girl's forehead as the Healer had instructed, wiping away her sweat. The girl shivered, her eyes open and staring off into the sky above, looking, Phariayh knew, at nothing but the visions in her head. She had spent most of the night crying out about beasts and demons pursuing her, ravings of the fever and flux. There were three other girls in Fush's tent, covered in the bedding they had to spare—Fush's generosity to the ill had stopped at giving up his own camp bed and sheets—though none were as ill as the girl Phariayh was attending to. She would not last the night, Phariayh was quite certain, having helped three other women to their ancestors' arms in the last days.

At first they had refused her care, refused to befouled by her touch, but as more and more had fallen to the plague, they had relented. There was no one else to turn to, especially with those who remained healthy out among the men, tending to the duties of those who were unable, and their presence in the sulihers quarantine forbidden. The Healer only came to the followers camp to see to them out of kindness. Phariayh was still not wanted there, though she supposed if enough of Fush's women grew sick, the men would grow desperate enough to seek her out as well. That was assuming she herself did not fall ill. So far, ancestors were on her side.

As Phariayh applied the cloth to her neck, the girl's eyes flashed open and stared in horror at her. "The beast," she cried out. "Somebody save me. Please."

Her voice was mournful, as though she expected no aid to arrive, and indeed, none of the others stirred from where they lay. Outside she could hear Fush yelling at one of the other women to hurry and finish her task. Phariayh reached out to adjust the blanket the woman had thrown off, only to have her seize her hand. "Spare me, I beg of you."

"Do not fear. Your ancestors are with you," Phariayh murmured. *And soon they will take you from this suffering*, she thought but did not say. The visions passed and the girl subsided back into sleep, a calm settling over her face that made her look very young. Phariayh studied her face, thinking about the fact that the two of them were of an age. The others had been too. It did not bear thinking of.

As she dwelled on it, unable to stop herself, Fush entered the tent and came over to where she sat, looming over her, his rasping breath filling her ears. He sounded labored, and Phariayh briefly wondered if he had fallen ill, and was unable to stop herself from offering a fervent invocation to her ancestors that it be so.

"The emissary has summoned you," Fush said, staring at her.

Something in the way he was looking at her, the strange, unreadable expression on his face, made her uncomfortable, and she felt a twinge of fear tremble up her spine. "Am I to go?" she said, glancing over at the girl she was tending to.

"Someone must earn coin and repay their debts. Evidently my ancestors so despise me that it is to be you."

Phariayh stood, knowing better than to reply, and nodded, turning to go. "I wonder what it is that he sees in you," Fush said, and Phariayh, knowing that this required a response, stopped at the tent's threshold.

"I don't know. He has not said."

The sutler stared at the three women who had fallen to the plague before turning to her with eyes that were filled with fire. "I am sure he has not," he said. His tone implied otherwise, and there was such an undercurrent of fury in his voice that Phariayh practically ran from the tent, cold with fear.

•••

After the first two days at Uigahel, when the fear of a Shadow Men attack had been foremost in the minds of everyone, the talk among the ranks turned to flux and its cause, with most agreeing that the emissary, that ancestor-less Enir who had forsaken all that was sacred on this plain, was involved in some way. He has used his alkemya to spread the flux amongst us, someone would say, and there would be many nods of agreement and grim talk of what needed to be done. That he had been seen at the river doing something to the water and had lied about what he had been doing, according to those who had been present when Masiph den Ibrazol, quadra jetthir, had confronted him about it, only further confirmed their suspicions.

There was a great debate as to why he was poisoning them and whom he was in league with. Some said it was obviously a Craitolian plot—he was the Qraul's emissary, after all—and that they were preparing an invasion of the Empire and wished the Renians to squander their forces in the desert. Others said the Craitolians were in league with the Enir Republics, for the emissary was Enir, after all, with the design of weakening the imperial army so that the Republics could further bleed the Ad Eselte of treasure by having to enlist the services of the Enir mercenary companies. But as the days passed and the plague spread mercilessly, with more than a third of the army falling to the flux, the emissary's dalliance with the Shadow came more and more to fore of everyone's thoughts.

Who was to say the man was even an Enir or the Qraul's emissary? It was known Adepts could disguise themselves, just as the Shadows could. That he could fool the Ad Eselte and Imperial Vazeir was no surprise; they had spent the summer obsessed with finding enemies hidden among the Nohritai, instead of noticing the one they had invited to their chambers. Now they were left to pay for their rulers' foolishness in blood, which was the lot of all sulihers, they knew, especially those sent into the desert. But as the days passed and the flux grew worse and worries about the food that remained began to creep into some of their minds, whispers began that something would have to be done.

On the fifth day at Uigahel, someone did. Two men stole into the sutler Fush's tent, looking for the demon woman. She was not there, and they found only three woman struck by the flux, and the sutler himself. They shook him awake and demanded that he tell them where the Shadow was.

"The emissary summoned her," Fush said, his breathing

laborious and his voice still heavy with sleep. "If she is not here, she must be with him."

The two sulihers looked at each other in the darkness, both hesitant to proceed. Launching a nighttime raid upon an Adept, particularly one with his Shadow familiar at hand, was beyond what they had envisioned when they had stolen from their quadra's camp, their thoughts quickened by a shared bottle of mehcuil. "Why did you bring a Shadow into our midst sutler?" one of the men said when the silence had lingered for too long and doubt began to intrude past the mehcuil.

Fush was confused and then frightened as the reality of what was taking place settled upon him. "She was the only one available. I tried. She is slave, nothing more."

"It is because of you that we have been poisoned," the man said, which seemed to decide the matter for the two of them. Justice would be served well enough by dealing with the sutler, and the emissary and his Shadow would surely understand the message being sent.

They dragged Fush protesting from his bed, and, as he screamed and cried out, waking half the camp, they carved the marks of treason and evil upon his forehead. That done, they cut his throat, dragged him to where the slaves had hobbled the ardehs and left him there to bleed to death, slipping away into the darkness.

It was some time before anyone on watch made their way over to the sutler's camp and discovered Fush's body, and by then he was dead. The watch sent word to Chisin, who sent some men to search the area, but by that time the two intruders had melted into the darkness and made their way back to their quadra.

The next day Gheyuth condemned the murder of the sutler before an assembly of the quadras, demanding that the guilty parties reveal themselves and accept the punishment due them. No one stepped forward, and there were many who whispered to their fellows that whoever had committed the deed had done the work the Vazeir had been unwilling or unable to do. Someone needs to do the same to the emissary, they said, for it was clear that he had bespelled the Vazeir and his staff. Something had to be done, everyone agreed, before it was too late and the flux had them all.

•••

The screams and the brief tumult that had followed them had awoken Vyissan during the night, and the thought of them returned to his mind as he rose that morning, filling him with trepidation at the sight of the sunlight stealing in through the shadows. The girl Phariayh lay nestled beside him, still asleep, her breathing soft. He had insisted she stay the night with them, though she had wanted to go, saying there were women ill with the flux she had to attend to.

"They will still be there come morning," he had said, refusing to let her escape his embrace. "And if not, their ancestors will be there to guide them to the next plain."

And so she had stayed the night, sleeping at his side. Now, with a new day upon him, and the screams of the night before still to be explained, he could not have said why it had mattered to him that she stay. There had been no reason to it. It was, in fact, the height of madness that she was even here to begin with, given the plague and all the rumor and insinuation that had accompanied it. But it seemed the more he was accused of conspiring with her and of being in league with the Shadows, the more he was drawn to her, compelled to seek her out, risking both their lives.

The Gods alone knew why, he thought, as he dressed himself.

"Are you awake, emissary?"

The Hjai's voice, heavy and abrupt, started Vyissan from his thoughts. The Renian did not wait for a reply, stepping into the tent, catching Vyissan still fumbling with his robes. Vyissan saw him taking in the whole scene without expression, his eyes coming to rest upon Phariayh, who had been wakened by his entrance and had lifted her head up to see who had entered. She immediately cast her eyes to the ground, an expression of subservience intended to disguise whatever she was feeling that Vyissan had noted in her before. He thought she looked frightened, though, and he could well imagine why. Likely she had never been in the presence of a more powerful Renian.

"How may I serve you, Husem?" Vyissan said, clearing his throat and gesturing for Chisin to sit. The Hjai remained where he was, towering over the Disciple, intending, it was plain to see, to intimidate.

"There was a murder last night," Chisin said, and Vyissan

nodded, remembering the screams that had disturbed his sleep. "Two men came into the sutler Fush's tent and killed him."

The Hjai was looking at Phariayh as he spoke, and Vyissan followed his gaze. The girl's expression did not change. "The men were looking for the Shadow," Chisin said, gesturing at Phariayh, "according to one of the girls who was in there. When he told them she was with you, they decided to kill him instead."

"Surely you don't think she is to blame, Husem?" Vyissan said.

"I do not think anything, emissary, I am merely informing you what has occurred. The Vazeir is deeply concerned by this murder. He feels it could lead to more violence, perhaps even to mutiny. The men feel that you and the girl are to blame for the flux."

"And what does the Vazeir think, Husem?" Vyissan could not stop the anger from entering his voice. Gheyuth had done nothing, as far as he could tell, to counter the rumors and innuendo about himself. Based on what he had said to Vyissan, he was sympathetic to those who suspected him of conspiring with the Shadows, and he had let those thoughts fester in an army where men were forced to watch their fellows die horribly to no purpose, not knowing whether they would be next.

"The Vazeir will do his duty, emissary, just as you will."

"I am glad to hear it."

The Hjai ignored the acid in his tone. "In the meantime, you would be well advised to remain in your tent and to stay on your guard. I am afraid we can no longer guarantee your safety in the camp. But I expect you have the means to protect yourself."

Vyissan did not rise to that bait. "The men you have provided will surely prove worthy of your confidence in the event something happens, unlikely as that is. If there is anything I can do to assist the Vazeir, Husem, please tell him I am at his service."

"I will be sure to let him know," Chisin said. He glanced at Phariayh and seemed about to say something more, but bowed instead and took his leave.

Vyissan did not need him to speak to know what the Hjai had been thinking. Phariayh's presence here was a danger to him, now more than ever, and if he were wise he would end his association with her now. To continue to see her now that blade had been put to flesh, with the promise of more violence to come, would be to confirm to everyone who harbored suspicions of them that they were in league. He had to end this madness, he realized, now, before they both were killed. Whatever misgivings about this war he might harbor, he would do no one—not Cepedutherupt, not the Qraul, not even the Renians who might be plotting to murder him—any good dead.

He watched as Phariayh climbed from the bed and put her own robes on, keeping her back to him as she did it, though it did little to halt the hunger he felt for her, which seemed insatiable.

"It would be best, I think, if you were to go," he said when she had turned to face him, her eyes downcast and vacant as they had been before Chisin. He was surprised how much it hurt to see that. "If we are seen together, it will bad for both of us."

The words sounded hollow in his ears.

"Yes, emissary," she said without emotion. He reached out to put a hand in her hair one last time, but thought better of it, and before he could think of anything else to say she was gone.

•••

The day that followed Fush's murder was filled with tension as the Hjai Chisin led an investigation and went from quadra to quadra demanding answers. Each jetthir was told to speak to his second and those others he most trusted in his unit to make preparations in the event that violence broke out among the lower ranks. As Chisin said to all of them, "It will begin with the Shadow and the emissary, but even if they should fall it will not satisfy their need for blood, because the flux will still be there. And they will turn to us next, so be on your guard. Any signs of dissent should be reported to me immediately. They cannot be tolerated."

Masiph was filled with trepidation at the Hjai's words. If there was a mutiny, as seemed increasingly likely with the way events were proceeding, he felt certain he would be one of the first jetthirs to fall. Nustef still clung to life in the fortress with the rest of the plague-ridden, and none of the others in his quadra trusted him. They all saw him, even Duhalleh, the man he had promoted to second in Nustef's absence, as nothing more than a Nohritai playing at war, given rank of jetthir without earning it.

Of course, all the officers were viewed like that, more or less, because there was some truth to it. Very rare was the man who rose through the ranks to become jetthir. But because Masiph was so new to the quadra, elevated mere days before the army had left

Darrhyn, he had been given no opportunity to prove himself to these men. He knew how difficult that could be; a year on the Watch had not done anything to his standing among the men.

Here it was no different. They saw a boy, a fool at play. Without Nustef at his side, he felt adrift and ill at ease among them, afraid of every word and step he made. His attempt to gain their favor by confronting the emissary had proved a disaster. Gheyuth had been furious, calling Masiph to his tent to tell him never to attempt such a thing again, and the men in the quadra had been strangely unimpressed, as if they had seen through his act. His anger had been real enough—he could not believe his father had formed an alliance with the Craitolians and their Adepts, no matter his excitement at a war in the desert—but they had sensed somehow the emptiness of the gesture. For all his bluster he had been waiting, hoping, for the emissary to flee or for someone like the Hjai to come and end the confrontation.

And Chisin had made certain to underline the connection between Masiph and the emissary, which every man would have known. He would forever be beneath his father's shadow here. Every man who died of the flux or at the hands of the Shadow Men was a result of a decision his father had made. If the emissary was in fact in league with the Shadows and had poisoned them with his magicks, Masiph knew that men would turn to him to exact their vengeance for his father's choices.

Worst of all, he was sure men from his quadra had been the ones to murder the sutler. They had not been on watch that night, and a few of the men had shared several bottles of mehcuil and had played dice and talked until well into the night. Masiph had stayed with the men for a time, but retired early, having duties to see to in the fortress first thing in the morning.

He woke some time later needing to piss, and when he left his tent he saw that the fire had died down to embers and the men had all gone to bed, except for two, Yuluir and Juihlran, the carrier. He could tell because he knew where everyone slept, those of rank closer to the fire, and both their spots were empty. At the time he had thought nothing of it, assuming they were at the latrines, and he did not think of it again until the next morning when word came of the murder. He had been the only one at the latrines and he had not met either man on the way there or the way back.

He had not mentioned anything to Chisin, and both men had

said they had slept with the others the night before. The Hjai's investigation would turn up nothing, he knew; even if he mentioned their absence, both men could easily invent some excuse to plausibly explain where they had been. Implicating them would only alienate the quadra from him further and make very plain his links to the emissary. Why, then, did he feel as though he were betraying himself in doing it?

If Nustef were here, he might speak to him of it. He had always been levelheaded in his counsel. He had almost mentioned the entire affair to him that morning, after the visit by the Hjai to the quadra, but his friend was still too weak from the flux. Masiph could not bear to so burden him as he struggled for his life. Each day he looked worse, and Masiph felt sure that it would not be long before his ancestors took him to the higher plains.

The rest of the day passed without incident, the entire camp seeming to be subdued, with little of the raucous laughter and song that still marked the army's days, even in the face of the plague. Everywhere Masiph went it seemed there were men at each other's ears in whispers, as though everyone could sense they were on the very precipice of some conflagration. Masiph felt it as well, the watchful eyes upon him wherever he went, knowing that he would stand with Gheyuth and the emissary.

"Ancestors, please spare us this madness," he whispered to himself on more than one occasion.

He went and did his afternoon rounds within the fortress, unable to banish thoughts of what might come once the sun set from his mind. There seemed to be fewer men within than in days past; he even spotted some empty beds. He mentioned it to the Healer, who nodded sadly and said, "Yes, a great many left to higher plains last night." Nustef, when he stopped by to see him, was asleep, and Masiph did not have the heart to wake him.

His quadra was on watch duty that evening, so he left the fortress to a hurried supper as the sun descended, and went to stand first watch. He stood by the sentry post on the river's far side, scanning the vast desert plain where darkness was taking hold, the cooling embers of the dying sun slowly fading. Duhalleh was with him; Masiph had wanted him there in case anything happened that evening. He needed to know which side the man was on. They were both silent and, Masiph thought, ill at ease, watching the empty desert and waiting for what the night would bring.

16

The light was nearly gone from the sky when Donier and Becir relieved the men on watch atop the hill overlooking the desert. Soon they would be swallowed in the night, unable to see beyond the outcropping of rocks they now stood on to the vast and unimaginable emptiness that lay beyond. Donier could not help but think of the dreams that had haunted him through the season, and the emptiness and silence that had marked them. The Gods had been speaking to him, and now he was certain that he understood their meaning, though the valley was nowhere to be seen.

The tolotes had begun to utter their cries with the encroaching darkness. The hills were full of them, though no Shadows had been sighted. A few cohorts had sent men out hunting and had managed to kill a few antelope further up the river. Donier's had not been one, which had led to a great deal of grumbling and complaining amongst the men who were forced to subsist on the disgusting gruel provided by the sutler.

There was no word from any of the Gvers as to when they might be marching again, though they had been within the hills for three days. Something, Donier was certain, had gone very wrong with the Renians. Rumors were rampant, though Ludenn had told him not a whisper had come from the Gvers or any of the Adepts about the reason for the delay. That, in many ways, was the most ominous sign of all.

His concern did not lay there tonight though, Donier thought, as he glanced at Becir. No, his concern tonight lay here with this man. One way or another, this would end here atop the hill. Donier would see to that.

Becir had complained bitterly about being put on watch with him again, saying that they should not be seen together so close to the assassination attempt.

"We have every reason to be seen together. We share a cohort and a watch," Donier had told him. "Besides, there is much we need to discuss."

He had also told him that he had requested an audience with Keleprai, which had set him somewhat at ease, his eyes shining with excitement. Donier had done no such thing, and had no intention of doing so anytime soon, but Becir did not need to know that. As they both settled into the watch, scanning the fading horizon and waiting for Senteur's heavens to grant them some light, Donier began. "What do you have to tell me?"

Becir shifted uncomfortably beside him. "There is nothing to tell. As I said, I will handle the distraction. It is up to you to do the rest. If you don't, I will see that you pay the price for your intransigence."

"As I have told you," Donier said in a level voice, "I will not act until I know more. If you will not tell me, I will not be killing the Gver in our audience—I will be telling him about you."

Becir laughed darkly just a tolote gave a mournful howl. "If I am executed, it is of no consequence. You will still have to carry out your duty to the Veil or your life will be forfeit, the others will see to that."

"I find that doubtful," Donier said.

"Whatever you think does not matter, the knife will still be at your throat should you fail to act."

"Who is going to put it there, Becir? I have yet to meet these compatriots you speak of, and I have seen no evidence they exist."

"You are a fool. The Veil is everywhere. We have infiltrated all parts of the Realm." There was a quiver in his voice as he spoke, though he tried to hide it.

Donier smiled, slipping his hand with his robe. "The Veil may have, but you have no allies here. The cohort has been watching you since we camped here, and you have spoken to no one. You have planned no disruption. You were going to send me to my death and hope that you could escape the executioner's hand. Do you think we are all fools?"

There was no reply from Becir, and Donier could hear him lunging forward in the dark, no doubt with dagger in hand. He was ready, though, had been expecting it, and stepped aside, catching Becir by the arm as his momentum carried him past. He plunged his own blade, which he had slipped from his robes, into the man's shoulder near his neck. Becir shouted in pain and cursed him, flailing his free arm, which also held his dagger, while trying to free himself from Donier's grasp. Donier tried to jerk his own blade free and plunge it into Becir's throat, but as he pulled the blade from the man's shoulder, Becir caught him with his flailing knife, cutting deep into his forearm.

Donier gasped at the sting of dagger and dropped his own to the ground before he had time to think. He swore and fumbled for the sword at his side, feeling the disturbing warmth of his blood as it ran down his arm and between his fingers. It hurt to grasp the sword, but he ignored it, trying to stay alert to where Becir was. It was hard to see anything even with a clear sky and the half-moon, but he could hear the other man's labored breathing, and he moved warily toward it with his sword raised.

They both caught a glimpse of the other at the same moment, darkness suddenly giving way to form, and swung wildly, Donier with his sword and Becir with his dagger, both missing their mark and nearly falling away to the ground. Donier spun around, lunging with his sword and ducking at the same time, managing to miss Becir again. It would be ludicrous if the situation weren't so desperate. The pain in Donier's arm was growing, the wound still bleeding heavily, and he knew that he needed to end this battle quickly before he weakened grievously.

Becir seemed to be thinking the same thing, for he charged at Donier, catching him unawares and knocking him to the ground. Donier gasped as the air went out of his chest. The sword had fallen from his hand and he reached out for it, finding only the rocky ground, while he frantically tried to take another breath. He said a quick invocation to Melinon to spare him, for it seemed certain that these were his final moments in this realm.

Becir fell on him, putting a hand to his throat and raising the dagger up, ready to finish him. His face was so near that Donier could just make out his fierce expression. "I told you your life was forfeit if you did not obey my word," Becir said, unable to resist a parting word.

As he spoke, Donier acted, smashing his forehead into Becir's nose, while simultaneously grasping the softness of his groin and twisting as hard as he was able to. He could feel the bone of the nose give way under his blow and felt blood begin to spatter on his face, while Becir began to scream and thrash as he tried to escape his grasp. Too late Becir remembered his dagger and tried to stab Donier, who had already grasped his arm with his free hand.

Before the man could regain any advantage, Donier used a burst of strength to flip him on his back, pinning the hand with the dagger to the ground while still twisting for all he was worth. Becir was frantic, screaming and clawing at him with his free hand, trying to shake loose Donier's grip. He ignored the man, smashing his forehead into his face again, leaving him stunned and Donier blinking away his own momentary dizziness.

When he had recovered, he turned his attention to the hand that still clutched the dagger, beating it against the ground until at last Becir released it. He moaned incoherently as Donier seized the dagger. Without a moment's hesitation, Donier cut his throat, a geyser of blood bursting from the veins to cover his face and his robes. Repulsed, Donier rolled off him, spitting the blood from his mouth and wiping it from his eyes. Beside him, Becir began to convulse and gasp for air, his hands reaching out as though to draw someone into an embrace.

Donier watched as the life slowly drained from him, and then dragged the man down the slope in the direction of the main camp. He drew Becir's sword from his belt and threw it aside after marking it with a little of his own blood. The dagger he cleaned and returned to Becir's sleeve. Returning atop the hill, Donier searched for his own weapons and replaced them in his belt and robe. That done, he tore a strip from his robe and tied off his own wound as best he could, and set off down the hill into the desert. When he reached the bottom of the hill, he sat down and rested, letting the cool air dry the sweat from his exertions, unable to stop himself from smiling.

He stayed there until the watch turned, Ludenn and another man coming to replace him. He could hear their approach, the offer of the password with no response and the rising panic in Ludenn's voice as he ordered the other man back to rouse the camp. Only then did Donier rise to sprint up the hill, arriving wild-eyed and out of breath just as the alarm was being sounded.

"Who goes there?" Ludenn said, his voice sounding high and strained.

"Melinon's whoreson," Donier said, the blasphemous password for the cohort.

"By the Gods," Ludenn said, "what happened?"

"We were set upon. I think he was as surprised as we were. He got me in the arm," he said, holding it up, only to realize that in the darkness Ludenn would have no way of seeing it. "And then he ran. I went after him and sent Becir to raise the army. Why has it taken so long for you to arrive?"

"Becir never came," Ludenn said.

"No," Donier said, with almost too much emotion.

Ludenn seemed not to notice. "We will need the torches," he said, his voice grim. "There will have to be a search. You are certain there was only one?"

"No," Donier said. "It seemed only one man, but who is to say? Neither of us heard anyone approach."

Ludenn did not reply, and they watched as torches blinked into existence in the camp, and then began to make their way, weaving through the darkness toward them.

17

Phariayh stood outside the tent watching as the last glimmers of light vanished from the sky, leaving only the stars and moon above, sentinels in the night. A breeze, cool and sweet, touched her face, and she closed her eyes to savor it. Quiet seemed to hang over everything in the camp, the men huddled around their fires talking in low murmurs. It could not help but seem sinister to her; the solemnity was so unlike the regular state of affairs in the camps, even through the worst of the flux, with the men joking and gaming and whoring to all hours. Tonight, though, she could tell would be different. Everyone seemed to sense it.

It was not safe for her here, a voice kept whispering in her head—she should flee into the desert, escape before the men who had killed Fush could finish what they had started with her. That was madness, though, she knew. It would only confirm the worst of their suspicions. They would hunt her down and see her punished, if the Shadows did not finish her first. She had to remain here and hope that the sparks that continued to alight here did not turn to fire.

There was a cry from within the sutler's tent, and she returned inside to look upon the patients there. Only two remained; the girl who had been raving the night before when the emissary had summoned her had passed to the plains beyond. The two who were left would join her soon, Phariayh thought—they seemed to have lost a great deal of strength in the last day, their end no doubt hastened on by the terrible shock of seeing Fush murdered before their eyes. She tended to the girl who had cried out, fever racking her thoughts, her eyes unseeing, putting a cloth to her head and neck to wipe away her sweat. There was nothing else to be done for either of them. They could not even keep water down.

Kagehell stepped into the tent behind her, his glowering face shrouded in the dancing shadows, the light from the lantern fitful as always. He had been Fush's second and was now the sutler, though he did not hold their debts. Such a thing did not matter out here, she knew; he owned them until they returned to Darrhyn, where Fush's partners would take charge. As much as she had despised Fush, wishing him to oblivion each time he had climbed atop her, his weight and dampness disgusting her, she knew this man was much worse. He would not take her to bed—he would whip her instead. He had already struck one girl for failing to carry out his orders with sufficient haste.

Phariayh could feel his gaze upon her, could sense the wrath that lay behind it, and so did not turn to face him, keeping her attention on the girl she was attending to, hoping, in vain, that he would leave her be.

"There is no point to this work," he said. "These two will not live out tomorrow. You should be with the others, out with the men, earning your keep."

Phariayh turned to look at him, unable to speak, not knowing what to do, her limbs heavy with dread.

"You heard me," Kagehell said when she did not move. "Your job is with the men. If you return empty-handed, you'll taste the whip."

The cloth that she was using to wipe the girl's brow was clenched tight in her hands. She set it down. "They will kill me," she somehow managed to say. Kagehell smiled, and Phariayh had to turn away so that she was not sick.

"Fush was too kind a master," he said, "taking his pleasure when he should have been showing you the whip. And what did it get him? I will not have you be the ruin of us here, though. If the men want your blood, they shall have it. Perhaps I can even charge for the pleasure of it. I'm sure there are a few men who would put coin to be the one to run a dagger through your demon heart."

Phariayh fell to her knees before Kagehell, tears blinding her, and began to beg him—there was nothing else she could do—in a forlorn and pitiful voice. "Please, I will do anything for you.

Anything. But don't send me to my death."

Kagehell was unmoved by her pleas. He seized her by the hair and dragged her from the tent. Phariayh screamed and sobbed, fighting against him to no avail. It felt as though her scalp was about to be torn off.

"Fush never broke you properly," Kagehell said. "You need to be taught that obedience is necessary for a beast."

He dragged her to where the ardeh were hobbled for the night, and Phariayh was certain he was going to kill her then and there. Her whole body seemed to go numb, while her soul floated above, waiting for its release.

He did not kill her. Instead, he seized one of the halters for the ardeh and put it roughly on her head, cinching it tight about her neck. "Please," Phariayh said, unsure of what she was even pleading for. She could not breathe, her sobbing overwhelming her, shaking her entire body.

"Now to your duty," Kagehell said with a laugh. "They say you can lead an ardeh to water, but it will not drink. We'll see if the same is true of you. I suspect not."

He jerked the halter viciously, lifting her up so violently she felt airborne before stumbling to the ground. He continued on, yanking and dragging her as he went. It took several attempts for Phariayh to regain her own footing, and in the meantime her face was cut and bruised by the hard ground, her hands torn in some brambled scrub. Even after she found her feet, Phariayh found it difficult to stay on them, as Kagehell would pull the halter at various times, sending her to the ground again.

As he neared the main encampment, where most of the quadras were settled, the men still up and huddled around their fires, Kagehell began to call out, "Gentlemen, the beast is here for your pleasure. Justice can be served at last. What would you have done with her?"

There were calls and shouts for her to be ravished or strung up from various quadras, though most fell silent at the command of their jetthirs. Only a few men dared to leave their fires and gather around Kagehell, most of them flush with drink. One threw a rock that struck Phariayh in the chest, causing her to gasp and cry out, to everyone's laughter. Others followed suit, kicking and punching at her until she fell to the ground and held up her hands, begging for mercy.

"Shall we give her mercy?" Kagehell shouted, as he yanked her back to her feet. Phariayh crouched unsteadily, tasting blood in her mouth, her one eye already swelled shut, the world dim and blurred.

A course of nos followed Kagehell's question, and he responded, "What shall we do to her?" Various suggestions were offered, including killing her, trying her for treason and several forms of intricate torture. The discussion of the merit of these was interrupted by the appearance of Vazeir Gheyuth and the Hjai Chisin and their guard, all with swords drawn and shields raised.

"Sulihers, what is going on here?" Gheyuth said.

"We are seeing justice done as it should have been days ago!" Kagehell cried, jerking the halter again so that Phariayh was spilled to the ground. She scrambled and looked pleadingly in the direction of the Vazeir.

"Be silent, sutler," the Vazeir said. "You are not being spoken to."

"I speak for everyone here," Kagehell said. "This madness has gone on long enough."

"Another word and your tongue will be removed," Chisin said with such force that Kagehell quailed and was silent.

"The rest of you should disperse immediately," said the Vazeir, raising his voice so that most of the camp would be able to hear him. "Anyone who remains will be considered as mutinous, and punished as such. If this woman is deserving of punishment, I will hear your petition tomorrow morning. We are not savages; we do not murder people at the whim of some sutler. Any attempt to harm either her or the emissary will be considered a direct contravention of my orders, and therefore treason. We all know the punishment for that."

There was an awkward silence, in which the sulihers who had gathered around Phariayh and Kagehell looked at each other warily, as though trying to determine how they might extricate themselves from what was suddenly a very uncomfortable situation with their honors intact. Kagehell would have none of it.

"You do not get to decide how the beast is punished," he said. "Her debts are mine, and I shall determine what punishment befits her crime."

Before he had a chance to continue, Chisin stepped forward and swung his shield at Kagehell's head. The edge caught him at the temple, and he let out an odd gasp of air before falling in a heap to the ground. Released from his grasp, Phariayh did not hesitate, fleeing through the first opening she saw in the crowd that surrounded her. No one made a move to stop her, though she could hear angry shouts from several of the men. She did not pause in her flight, running blindly through the camp until she reached the open desert and was certain there was no pursuit behind her.

From there she gathered her thoughts and her breath. The shouts from where Kagehell had led her were growing louder, and she could hear what sounded like the ringing clash of weapons. The quadras, all of whom had remained fairly quiet during the earlier confrontation, seemed to spring to life, with torches being lit and orders being issued and arguments being made. Behind her, at the sentry posts, which she had almost stumbled upon in her flight, the men on watch lit torches and moved toward the growing tumult.

Phariayh watched these developments sick with fear. The army would soon be at war with itself, and there would be no safe place for her. Except for one, she realized, and she began to make her way to the emissary's tent.

•••

Vyissan spent an anxious day alone in his tent, pacing its narrow confines as the weight upon his chest grew. Every time he tried to force himself to sit and be still, his worry would overwhelm him and he would find himself up again, moving about, muttering to himself words that even he did not quite comprehend. It was the waiting for what was to come that was driving him mad. That and not knowing.

He expected more violence this night. Perhaps someone would grow daring enough to make an attempt on his life, but the shape and form it would take was still to be determined. The mood of the army would decide it, and, trapped as he was in this tent, he had no idea what the men were thinking and feeling. They had doubled the guard outside his tent, which told him what the Vazeir thought of the situation. It did not help to settle his nerves.

He had not sent to the High Adept today or the last two days. There was no point, he told himself, though he knew that was not the reason. That man had put him into this cauldron of wrath and hatred, all to what end? But he would not think of it. It did no good to dwell on such things. When nightfall came, he needed his mind clear to be ready to act.

Evening stole into the tent slowly, the shadows lengthening on the ground until at last he had to light a lamp to be able to see. The first sign that something was amiss came when no one arrived with his dinner. He had been hoping it would be Phariayh so that he might see that she was still fine. Next he heard a man shouting, and responses from a few others. He could not make out most of what was being said, but the words beast and justice did reach his ears, causing his stomach to lurch. Outside the tent he could hear the four guards drawing their swords and shifting about.

Before he knew what he was doing, he found himself standing before the entrance to the tent, clenching and unclenching his fists. The rage he felt was sudden and all consuming. He forced himself to sit down, unsure of what he might have been about to do, knowing no good could come of it. They could kill him easily. No matter what they believed of alkemya, he knew the truth of the art, and it was feeble when faced alone with a mob of angry men. His thoughts returned to those days upon the streets of Devew when beatings had been a matter of course, the result of finding oneself alone in the presence of Craitolians, and his rage returned. He had not thought he would feel so helpless again.

Phariayh's screams, dim but unmistakably in her voice, were what roused him to his feet and carried him outside the tent to where the guard stood.

"Back inside, emissary, this is no time to be about," one of the men snarled, jabbing him in the chest with his shield.

"Do not touch me," Vyissan said in a cold voice, pushing the shield aside and staring past the men. All four, as one, stepped away from him, eyeing him warily, unsure whether the greater threat lay with him or whatever was occurring across the camp.

"Sulihers, what is going on here?" Gheyuth's voice, hard and authoritative, carried above the din and to where they stood.

At his words, the guards seemed to remember themselves, and they turned from Vyissan to face the growing confrontation. Looking past them, Vyissan could see the torches of Gheyuth's men as they moved to surround those already gathered. He could see little beyond torchlights, various moving shapes that might be humans, though he tried to pick out Phariayh, who was lost somewhere in their midst.

"Emissary, please return to your tent," one of the guards—not the man who had confronted him earlier—said, almost pleading with him. "Nothing good can come of this."

Vyissan nodded, knowing the man was correct, and returned within, where he sat on the edge of his flimsy bed and held his head in hands. The next minutes were excruciating, as he listened to the shouts of two men. Gheyuth was one, Vyissan was certain. These were followed by a brief and ominous silence, which erupted into a tumult of noise a moment later. One of the guards outside the tent swore, and another ordered him to be quiet. Vyissan thought he was going to be sick. He closed his eyes and began an invocation to Melinon, praying that he be spared the hand of madness that seemed to be touching everyone here who had somehow escaped the flux.

The cries seemed to grow louder and louder, Gheyuth's rising above everyone, ordering a calm which did not come. Swords had been drawn and blows were being exchanged, he could hear, and the guard were debating whether they should stay at their posts or go in aid of the Vazeir. Their words left Vyissan cold. If most of the army had turned against Gheyuth, they were doomed. He would be dead, and Cepedutherupt's grand dream of ridding the Shadows of the engines would end in disaster. All because of the flux and a girl with the wrong shade. The Gods laughed at their plans, made a mockery of them all.

It was impossible to tell whether the battle was growing nearer or simply engulfing the entire camp. Finally he decided he could no longer stand not knowing what was taking place just beyond the thin fabric of his tent. If his doom was here, he would see it with open eyes. The Gods would decide his fate anyway.

Outside, he saw the guard had moved away from his tent, though they still formed a sort of loose barricade around its entrance. They had lit torches and set them on poles on either side so that the light was cast wide. One of them glanced back as he stepped out. Their eyes met for a moment and Vyissan saw fear barely contained. He nodded at the man in what he hoped was a reassuring fashion, and the guard turned back to watch the growing struggle.

As near as Vyissan could tell in the darkness, the mutineers had overwhelmed Gheyuth's forces, their ranks swelling with men from the nearest quadras. Still, he thought, based on the numbers he could discern, most of the men remained uncommitted, refusing to attack their fellow soldiers. That gave him heart: if the majority stood apart, awaiting the triumph of the victors, the situation could still be won, provided Gheyuth had the men to beat back the rebellion.

At the moment that was not the case. His guard was soon forced to flee beyond the camp to where the sentries were posted. The mutineers shouted in triumph, yelling declarations of freedom, and were joined by a few others from among the bystanders who decided that the battle had been won. These newcomers were cheered until one suliher managed to shout above the din, "Let us finish the emissary while our ancestors favor us, and free ourselves from his poison."

There were shouts of assent and the crowd began to move toward them. Vyissan could hear one of the guard let out a yelp of fear, but to their credit, none of the four fled at the mutineers' approach. Perhaps they were paralyzed by fear, Vyissan thought—certainly he was, all his being crying out that he should flee into the desert while time still remained.

As he watched, unable to look away, the mutineers approach, a movement at his side caught his eye and he whirled to face this new threat. There was a curse on his lips, and he reached out for all the astral he could grasp. He would see their fear justified. A shape materialized from the darkness and then a face, and he looked on heartsick and in horror. It was Phariayh.

18

The High Adept looked haggard and drawn, his eyes red from exhaustion and worry. Keleprai found himself wondering when last the man had slept, knowing it must have been days. Not since they had come to these hills to camp, at least, he thought. Since they had arrived, Cepedutherupt had given no word of any change in their situation, offered no guidance as to when they might expect to march again, all while their food dwindled, the men grew restless and the Shadows waited.

If the situation were not so desperate, Keleprai would have been tempted to say that this had been at the root of all his fears about the invasion. Too many had had the desert break them without ever facing the Shadows, and it seemed they would join them. There was no happiness in such thoughts, though, as evidenced by the agonized expression on the High Adept's face.

He had summoned them here, Keleprai and the boy Qraul, on the evening's edge as the men settled down in the growing darkness to their meals. It could only mean he had something to tell them. Some disaster had befallen the Renians and he could hide it no longer, for hard decisions would have to be made. Wine was poured for all of them, and when the attendants left, Cepedutherupt looked from Laterala to Keleprai and said, "I feel I must tell you I have not heard from Vyissan in two days. I expect the worst."

Silence lingered between them, Laterala looking unsure and frightened because of it. Keleprai felt his own fear, not because of whatever had happened to the Disciple and the Renians, but because he knew that Cepedutherupt would want them to carry on to Esyln, in the face of all reason. And he would expect Keleprai to stand with him.

"What has happened?" Keleprai said. Neither of them had touched their wine. Laterala looked from one to the other, utterly lost.

"The flux," Cepedutherupt said, and Keleprai felt his chest tightening. "They've had to stop and quarantine the infected to see if it willstop the spread."

"And it hasn't," Keleprai said. Half the army or more could be wiped out by such a plague, he knew, and those who survived could be too ruined to fight.

"It seemed to be working, though it was slow going. When I last heard from Vyissan, he thought it would not be long until they were on the march again. The problem is that I have not heard from him in two days."

"What do you think has happened?" Keleprai said, while he wondered whether the High Adept would have thought fit to inform them of the flux striking the Renians if Vyissan had not disappeared. He knew the answer, though. He would have continued with his plan, no matter that the Renians would only have half the force they had promised, willing to sacrifice them all in the name of alkemya.

"I cannot say. You know how the Renians feel about alkemya. He was fearful with the flux. Some blamed him for it."

Keleprai nodded, thinking that the Renians were a sensible people. Adepts were not to be trusted. Who knew what Cepedutherupt had promised them beyond the silk. He had probably said that the desert was theirs to take, never mind that the last thing the Realm needed was an empire at its border. The Shadows as they were, nomadic and tribal, offered little in the way of a threat, no matter what the High Adept might say.

"Can't you..." Keleprai made a vague gesture with his hand.

"No," the High Adept said. "We are still too far apart. I cannot feel him. I have sent to him, of course, numerous times. But there has been no reply."

"So you think he is dead," Laterala said, finding his voice at last. He finished his cup of wine at a gulp. Keleprai was tempted to do the same.

"It is impossible to say. He may be dead. He may be ill with the flux and without strength to send. He may be alive and well but constrained in some other way. There is no way for me to tell."

They were all silent, each of them mulling their thoughts. Keleprai spoke at last. "We should go back, return to Craitol."

"No," Laterala said.

"We cannot," the High Adept said in the same moment.

"We must," Keleprai said, "before it is too late. Even if the Renians do reach Esyln, they will be in no position to offer us anything in the way of support. Even the ones who survive the flux may still be shitting blood. And if we cannot overcome the Shadows alone, as you have said is the case, then we cannot overcome them with a flux-ridden army at our side."

"We must destroy the engines. The Shadows cannot be allowed the knowledge of alkemya."

"They have it," Keleprai said, slamming his fist on the table. "You can destroy every engine they possess—they will still have it. And I would venture to guess they will find a way to build others, no matter what you and the Council do."

Cepedutherupt stood, trembling with fury. "Have you listened to nothing that I have said these last years? Have I confided in you for nothing? The Shadows are on the precipice now, just as Kercubegahedd was. If we do not act, if we do nothing, they will have power to rival the Council. That cannot be allowed to happen. No matter what the cost to us, to this army, to our rule, we must shatter their reservoirs or they will overwhelm us. Kercubegahedd's minions will see to that. The Kragians will not rest until they have overthrown Craitol and the Council."

The High Adept had to pause to draw in some air. Laterala looked frightened, glancing from one man to the other. Keleprai could feel the heat in his cheeks, and he forced himself to take a sip of wine before he spoke.

"I have heard you. I have listened, old friend. But you have not listened to me. Even with the engines, the Shadow Men are not the threat you think they are. They have no kingdom, no empire. They are nothing but bands and tribes of thieves and miscreants and worse. If they have the engines and alkemya, they are as likely to use them against each other as against us."

"Kercubegahedd's minions will see that they attack us. Their war with us has not died out."

"Let them try," Keleprai said. "You cannot herd a Shadow. Meanwhile, if we are broken here in service to the Council's desires, what Realm do we return to? One where Pervelte a Pysel rules, I would venture."

"Never. I would die before that happens," Laterala said.

"Yes, I imagine we all would," Keleprai said, fixing the Qraul with a glare. The boy went pale at the thought, and Keleprai saw his hand begin to tremble.

Cepedutherupt had managed to regain his calm. He sat down again, staring levelly at Keleprai. "We will not turn aside from this battle," he said. "I will not allow it."

"Do you rule here now?" Keleprai said, filling his voice with derision.

The High Adept's eyes widened, as though he had only just realized what he had said. The trembling in Laterala's hand seemed to be growing worse, and Keleprai was afraid the boy would begin to cry. Cepedutherupt opened his mouth to speak, but his reply was cut short as shouts of alarm went up outside the tent. All three looked at each other in horror as they heard the cries: "The Shadows are here. We're under attack."

19

Masiph did not speak as the confrontation occurring behind them in the camp exploded with swords drawn amidst shouts and screams. He could not see what was happening—he did not want to see what was happening, and fervently hoped that Gheyuth and Chisin would be able to put down this insurrection before it spread and he was forced to act. Beside him, Duhalleh was very quiet and still. Masiph could not read his expression in the darkness, and hoped that his own unease and fear was not palpable.

Duhalleh heard the footsteps approaching before he did, and he whirled to face the intruder, drawing his sword as he did. Masiph found himself taking an involuntary step back, nearly stumbling in the darkness. He bit off a curse and seized his own sword, peering into the night for any shape that presented itself.

"Who passes here? Name yourself," Duhalleh called out into the darkness.

"It is me," came the response, very near, though Masiph still could not make anyone out.

"What is the password? The password," he said in a sharp voice. The man had been Renian and young. Yuluir, he was almost certain.

"Oh," the suliher said in surprise. "The alkemyst's familiars."

"Come forward," Masiph said, sure now that it was Yuluir. A moment later he came into view, Masiph giving thanks to his ancestors for the clear night and the half-moon.

"Why is your weapon drawn?" Duhalleh said with an edge to

his voice.

Yuluir, Masiph saw, had his sword in his hand raised as though he were ready to use it. Fear seized him as he remembered the suliher's absence while Fush had been murdered. Was he with the mutineers? Was this all part of some plot to remove them from the battle that seemed likely to come their way? The next moments were agonizing as Yuluir did not respond, seeming to stare at his weapon. Beside him, Masiph could sense Duhalleh tense with dread.

"Oh," Yuluir said again, and sheathed his sword.

"What are doing here, Suliher?" Masiph said, hoping he sounded commanding, though he very much did not.

"I...what are we..." Yuluir trailed off, unable to give voice to his thoughts.

"Not abandoning our posts during the middle of a mutiny," Duhalleh said.

"Yes," Yuluir said, exhaling loudly. "But what if..."

"If the Vazeir needs us, he will send for us," Masiph said. "For now, our concern is still the Shadows. Return to your post, Suliher."

There was a long pause, during which Masiph wondered if Yuluir was going to refuse his order, but in the end the youth said, "Yes, Husem," and ran back the way he had come.

Duhalleh whispered an invocation under his breath and said, "I nearly killed him."

"It would have been his fault."

"Even still, I would not have slept any easier."

"I know," Masiph said, turning back to the battle, which had lulled for a moment and now seemed to be growing. Unspoken between the two men was the seeming inevitability of the fight reaching them, and the necessity of putting their fellows to the sword. Masiph offered his own invocation to his ancestors to spare him from that nightmare, knowing it was too late and that the nightmare had already begun.

His fears became real moments later as the mutineers drove Vazeir Gheyuth and his guard from the camp. They both watched as the bobbing torches moved nearer until figures became visible beneath them. Masiph could see the Hjai Chisin, blood streaming down his face, yelling at various men, his words drowned out by the cheers of the mutinous sulihers. They, judging by the movement of their torches, were moving toward the emissary's tent. What would happen to their alliance with the Craitolians, he wondered, if their Adept was murdered here? Though, given the rumors he had survived a poisoning, who knew if a few dozen men armed only with swords would be able to harm him.

As Masiph contemplated the emissary's fate, Gheyuth appeared, detaching himself from the retreating force and moving swiftly toward he and Duhalleh, followed by a frightened-looking retainer carrying a torch.

"Jetthir," the Vazeir said as he came near, "do you stand ready?"

"I do, Husem," Masiph said immediately, and was glad to hear Duhalleh echo his words.

"Good. Summon your quadra to you. Any man who refuses will be executed. We will retake this camp before sunrise and see these whoresons get what they deserve."

"Yes, Husem," Masiph said, and, after hesitating a moment, added, "What of the watch?"

"Forget it. If we lose this battle tonight, it will not matter whether the Shadows attack. Gather your men."

Masiph did not need to be told twice, and turned to Duhalleh, motioning for him to follow. They went without torches, not wanting to draw attention to what they were doing, lest any of the mutineers or, ancestors forbid, the Shadows were watching. All the men came without issue, though Masiph could sense their fear. He tried to project a calm, failing miserably, he was certain, his voice sounding strained and nervous to his ears.

When they had completed their circuit of the camp and rejoined the Vazeir's guard, Masiph went to present himself to Gheyuth, who was watching Hjai Chisin as his wound was attended to.

Seeing him, Gheyuth put an arm around him in a fatherly gesture that only served to increase Masiph's nervousness. "How were your men?"

"They are all here," Masiph said.

"Good. How are they? Good men? They will stand in a fight?"

"I don't know," Masiph said, thinking that he did not even know if he could stand in a fight. His only experience had resulted in him being run through. The thought of that caused him to shudder and nearly go faint. The whole incident, only pieces of which he had been able to recall to that point, came rushing back to him in an instant. These were not Shadows he was facing, though, he told himself. They were his fellow sulihers. His stomach twisted at the thought.

Gheyuth squeezed his shoulder, pulling him closer, and whispered in his ear, "Take courage; you have faced worse than this and survived, do not forget. And your men are here, so they are committed now. If we lose we are all dead, they will know that."

Masiph nodded, trying to breathe and having difficulty doing so.

"Good. When we get into the camp, go to where the rest of your quadra is and summon the rest of your men. Tell them you and their fellows are risking their lives for this army. They will come too."

"Yes," Masiph said, though he felt none of the Vazeir's confidence.

"Good. Go to your men. As soon as the Hjai is ready, we march."

He said it with such fierceness that Masiph's fear of the mutineers and the battle to come vanished for the moment, replaced by terror of the man whose arm was around him. He knew then which side of the coming battle he wanted to side on, for Gheyuth would offer no mercy to any who stood against him.

•••

The horror Vyissan felt at seeing Phariayh was reflected in her face as she saw the approaching mob. She seemed paralyzed at the sight of it. Vyissan could hear rage-filled screams of recognition from the approaching sulihers as they caught sight of her as well. He tried to wave her away into his tent, but she seemed not to notice him, her eyes fixed upon the sulihers, their weapons drawn and threatening.

He went to her, hearing one of his guard swearing as he realized she was there. For some reason she had an ardeh halter on her head, and Vyissan took it off. His touch caused her to flinch. There were bruises and cuts on her face, and one eye had nearly swelled shut. He took one of her hands in his, holding tightly as she tried to jerk it away.

"Don't fear," he said, his own voice trembling. "Go to my tent.

It will be all right."

She did not seem to hear him, staying rooted where she was. Before Vyissan could try again to get her to move, one of the guards called out, "Emissary."

Vyissan whirled and saw half a dozen men charge at the four guards. Two fell immediately, and as he watched the last two in their futile struggle, he called out, "Stand aside. Throw down your swords. You can do nothing for me."

After a moment's hesitation, they both did, stepping back and throwing their swords to the ground to the cheers of the mob. Both retreated to stand beside him.

"We will not abandon you," one said.

"What use would your deaths be on top of mine?" Vyissan said. "Go while you can."

They both made to move away, but one of the mutineers shouted, "We will not spare them. They have betrayed their ancestors by standing with you."

"They have surrendered," Vyissan said.

"There shall be cleansing tonight," was the reply from another. "All you must die to free us from the flux."

"There will be a cleansing, but it will be all you who will perish at the hands of Gheyuth," one of the guard shouted in turn, his voice cracking with fear. He pointed toward the far side of the river, where Vyissan could see the Vazeir marshaling his forces. Presumably they would march soon upon the camp. Not soon enough, he thought.

A few of the mutineers turned to look as well, and a mutter of unease passed through the group. Several of the men glanced at each other, and Vyissan could see the doubt on their faces in the torchlight. A sliver of hope began to steal into his blood, warming his limbs, which had gone cold with terror. He dared to allow himself to believe the mob could be turned and splintered before their lives were taken.

Such dreams were shattered when someone in the crowd picked up a broken stone from one of the ruins and threw it at Phariayh. It struck her in the head and she fell, without even uttering a cry, and lay unmoving on the ground. Cheers erupted from the mob, their feeling restored, the moment of doubt now passed, and they began to advance upon Vyissan and the remaining guards, braying like animals in lust. Some of them began to beat upon their shields with their swords, as if they wanted Vyissan and the others to flee so that they might hunt them.

Vyissan looked upon Phariayh's prone form, the cuts and bruises upon her face and her torn skirt, and felt his wrath return. It seemed to form his whole being; he ached with anger, could barely see. All those Craitolians who had left him to his fate, broken and bloodied, returned to his vision, and he saw them advancing toward him, beating their swords against their shields. He had thought to escape their hate by joining the Council, but it had been no different there. His difference had marked him just the same, his success only more so.

Even joined to Cepedutherupt, his greatest triumph—how his heart had sung when he had been told—there had still been questions whispered when it was thought he couldn't hear, abrupt silences when he entered the room. He had never asked the High Adept why he had been chosen for such an honor. Cepedutherupt had never volunteered an answer. But Vyissan knew the reason why, had known it without ever admitting it to himself. It was not skill that had separated from the others, as he had told himself. It was the shade of his skin.

He was to be an example, proof that the Council and the High Adept had no hatred in their hearts for the northerners, even after the war with Kercubegahedd. They were still welcomed in the Council, just as they were welcomed in the courts of Craitol. Had the Qraul not married a northerner, after all? Was the High Adept's Disciple not a Kragian from Devew? What need did these people have to rebel now that they had been given so much?

He seethed with all this emotion that it seemed he could not longer contain. His entire existence seemed to surge up from within, years recalled in an instant, and then vanishing completely, leaving him empty. Somehow he was still holding the halter that Phariayh had been wearing, the rope almost cutting into his hand he was clutching it so tightly. He dropped it and turned to face the oncoming horde.

The men were still wary as they approached, no one moving too far forward from the others, fearing what he might be capable of doing. *Why don't I show you*, Vyissan thought, and began to form a seed of alkemy from whatever astral he could grasp from the nearby elements. It was something he did effortlessly, without thought, and when he had a germ of sufficient size ready, he began.

The first thing he did was to seize the two men nearest him, placing bonds of alkemy on them. They were both frozen where they stood, grimacing wildly as they struggled to break free. The men coming up behind them, not realizing what was happening, ran into them and sent them toppling to the ground. This startled those around the two bonded men, and they halted in their tracks, unsure whether their fellows were alive or dead and if a similar fate awaited them. A few made warding signs against evil.

One man, overcome by drink and rage, charged on with his sword raised, shouting a curse at Vyissan. He had already formed his next seed, and as the man came near he unleashed it upon him, sending it into his flesh. The seed of alkemy unbalanced the man's astral, transmuting it and him. He began to scream, an awful sound that silenced the rest of the mob, who had begun to cheer him on, as his body stiffened and started to twitch, like that of man suffering the touch of a demon. The stench of burned flesh began to spread and several of the mutineers stepped back, mouthing invocations to their ancestors. Many grabbed their heads or fell to their knees wretching, as the wave of alkemy reached them. They looked at each other in terror, some of them trying and failing to flee, their sense of equilibrium gone.

The man fell silent, though his mouth remained twisted in the form of an anguished cry. The stench of burned flesh was overwhelming now, reaching even beyond the mob and the guard to the rest of the army, and Vyissan could hear cries of fear rising up there. The man's eyes frantically sought Vyissan's, pleading with him for mercy. He offered none, continuing to pour the alkemy into him as fast as he could form it, until he saw the glimmer in the man's eyes disappear as the last of his mortal substance was destroyed.

As the man tumbled to the ground and Vyissan ceased to form the germ of alkemy, several of the others in the mob managed to find their footing, and fled from him, stumbling and weaving. They were met by the Vazeir's guard, with Gheyuth at the lead. Vyissan watched, still trembling with rage, exhausted by the effort of using so much alkemy, as every last one of the mutineers was put to the sword.

THREE:

NO WIND STIRS

20

The swelling had gone down enough that Phariayh was now able to see out of both eyes, and most of her bruises had turned from an ugly purple to a still grotesque yellow. Walking was still painful, and her neck still ached when she lay down to bed or with the emissary. She offered no protest in those moments, for the man had saved her life with his terrifying display of magick. It still seemed impossible to her that any man could paralyze others where they stood and burn them up from within, to say nothing of the awful sensation of the alkemya washing over her, seeming to tear at her very being, leaving her empty and without the feeling of a soul.

Ancestors knew she had no soul to speak of, or she would not have been punished so on this plain. At least they might have let her perish rather than let her live on like this, every day upon the precipice of death, whether from the army she was here to serve or from the other soulless ones who inhabited this desert. For now the emissary had insisted on her staying in his tent, so she could at least forgo her duties as a follower as the army began to march again.

On the march that day, the men had all eyed her warily, whispering to each other, as she had walked behind the emissary. She could not hear what they said, but she had no need to. They were, no doubt, calling her the emissary's familiar, the one who had facilitated his magicks on that terrible night, resulting in the deaths of so many of their fellows. That the Vazeir and his guard had done most of the killing, executing those who had risen in the mob, would be ignored. Nothing could be done about that, just as nothing could be done about the emissary or her, so long as he remained. Once that changed, though...the thought was best not finished.

For now things were quiet, the men subdued by the crushing of the revolt and the knowledge that they were nearer every day to confrontation with the Shadow Men. Their fear of the flux had dissipated with the plague seeming to have run its course. With a few exceptions, those who had fallen ill had either succumbed to the disease or recovered, and there had been no new infections in the past day, according to Atasem. The relief was palpable in the ranks, she thought, those who remained happy that they had come through the whirlwind that had seized everyone in those terrible days and now hoping that somehow they would survive the coming days and return home to the Empire.

That hope was not for her, though—her future was as obscure as the night she found herself looking out upon, clouds covering over the skies so that not a star shone through. She tried not to think of such things, to enjoy the evening's cool, a delightful respite after the heat of the day and the work of the march. Atasem had gone to meet with the Vazeir, for they expected to arrive at Esyln and rendezvous with the Craitolian army the day after tomorrow. Arrangements had to be made and agreed to, the emissary had told her, looking exhausted by the day's efforts.

He had looked drained of spirit since the night he had unleashed his alkemya upon the army, though he had insisted on putting the lie to that with her on the nights that followed. This night, she felt certain, would be no different. He had been seized by a fervor beyond reason which drove him to her arms, as though she had bespelled him. His fascination with her was as frightening, in its own way, as the hatred of Kagehell and others.

When Atasem returned, he ushered her inside his tent, saying, "You should take care, Phariayh. I fear it is still not safe here for either of us."

His concern made her angry, and she did not reply as he set the lantern on his table and turned its flame higher. It was his fault, his being here, an Adept in a land without, that had condemned her to this fate. However miserable her days might have been with Fush and the other women, it was no worse than anything she had endured before. That she had longed to become his familiar to escape that drudgery only made this present moment, when she wore the familiar's mask while accruing none of its benefits, all the worse.

Sensing her anger, Atasem sat on the edge of his bed and covered her hands in his own. "Tomorrow or the next day we will arrive at Esyln and things will begin. I will not be able to help you then—my Qraul will have other duties for me, and neither army will be happy at the sight of someone of your shade once the killing begins."

"What would you have me do?" she said, pulling her hands free and looking out of the tent at the darkness. It seemed to dance as the flame from the lantern quivered fitfully.

"In truth, I do not know. You will know better than I if you would be safe among the other women. They will have need of you with those that have died, no matter what they might feel."

"You will not take me with you? I cannot be your familiar?" she said, hating herself for the need in her voice she could not disguise.

"Oh, Phariayh," the emissary said. "I am sorry. It would do no good for you to follow me where I have to go. I will have to enter the cauldron, and I may not survive."

Something in his voice gave her pause. He did not sound like a man who returned to his masters willingly. He sounded like her, conflicted and desperate, faced with choices that offered little in the way of hope. It did not stand to reason. She had seen him take on an entire mob; it seemed impossible that anything could threaten him, let alone break his spirit. Yet he was different, she could see, his thoughts already casting forward to whatever fate awaited him. She would be forgotten, abandoned, just as her ancestors had abandoned her for the sins of her mother.

"I will not survive here," Phariayh said, her voice flat and without emotion. "They will kill me as soon as you leave."

"No, they will not," he said. "When I leave, the battle will have begun, and they will all be too busy to concern themselves with you. The women and the Healer will need your help with the wounded."

"The women will not want me near them. The wounded will not want me to touch them."

He shook his head. "Need will force them to accept you soon enough. And it will not be any different with my people. At least here you know the tongue."

He sounded confident, reasonable, though she could tell by looking at him that he was seeking to reassure himself as much as her. Anger shook her as she realized what drove his reluctance. He did not want his people to know about her. It was one thing for Renians to see him consorting with her and believing that she was her familiar, but if his own masters saw, it would be another matter altogether.

"You have to take me with you," she said, "after what you have done to me. They all think I am your familiar, and they blame us both for the death of their friends. If I stay, they will take the vengeance that should be yours to bear and put it upon me."

She could see the weight of what she'd said settling upon him. "Perhaps you are right. It would be best if you came with me, though I fear it will go little better for you with my people."

"There is nowhere in all the realms for me," she said with a fierceness that made him wince. The emissary nodded and took her hands again in his, a consoling gesture, and this time she did not pull them away.

•••

Esyln remained, after more than one hundred years, broken and torn asunder, a memory recalled in a nightmare. Here lay the death of the Empire, Gheyuth thought, as he looked at its fragmented wall and the hollowed-out structures that lay behind it, once the jewels of the desert, now the bones of a skeleton worn away by the wind and the sun. They were the first Renians to set eyes upon the city in over ninety years, and the Vazeir felt a stir of emotion at the thought. The flux had nearly broken them, but now they stood on the precipice of reclaiming their birthright.

First they had to deal with the Craitolians, who, if their emissary was anything to judge by, were hardly to be trusted. Gheyuth tore his gaze from the ruins and turned his attention back to the army that stood across from them, and glanced at Chisin. "What do you think?"

"Let's not waste any time, Vazeir," the Hjai said. "The sooner this is done with, the better."

Gheyuth resisted a smile. "Where is the emissary?"

The Hjai raised an eyebrow significantly, and Gheyuth turned to see the man approaching them. They had spoken only once since the night of the revolt, when the emissary had used his foul magicks, and though Gheyuth well knew the man had had little choice but to do so, it still angered him to have been exposed to such impure power. It was against all unity, all balance in this realm. There would be further desecrations to follow, for this army before them was filled with Adepts and other familiars of these dark arts, but at last he understood why Ibrazol and the Ad Eselte had risked forsaking their ancestors in this alliance. If they could regain the desert it might all be worth it—no matter the corruption they would all suffer on this plain, their ancestors would embrace them on those above.

The emissary bowed stiffly as he came before them and stood aside. "Shall we?" Gheyuth said, and received a nod in return. If the Vazeir could have put a word to the expression on the emissary's face as he faced his brethren for the first time in weeks, after having endured trials he must have feared surviving, it would have been *ambivalent*. The man was hesitant, almost reluctant, to go forward, which Gheyuth could not begin to understand after all that had transpired.

Gheyuth looked behind him to ensure that his herald and standard bearers were arrayed correctly, and that the men with the gifts for the Qraul from the Ad Eselte were ready. When he was satisfied that all was as it should be, he nodded at the Hjai, who called the party to order. The herald sounded his horn and was met in reply by a similar call from the party gathered across from them, and both sides began to march together.

It was startling as they came near enough to make out the faces of those opposed to them to see the red shade of the Craitolians. Gheyuth realized he had never seen a man of such of coloring before, had only read descriptions of them. They were not as red as he had imagined, but their dark beards were as variously formed as he had been told. In amidst the group of Craitolians he spotted a man who had to be one of their white-shaded northerners. Again the shade was not as he had envisioned it—it was just a lighter hue, although more yellow than red, if he had to put a color to it. The man's eyes were as dark as anyone's he had seen—as dark as the emissary's, in fact—and his hair was thick and black without the hints of red that the Craitolians had. All of them were resplendent in their Craitolian silks, colored red and blue and green, and hues that he had never seen created before.

He realized he was gawking, and forced himself to stop, realizing for the first time what a disadvantage he was at in this moment. The Enir had lived among them for centuries; they were used to shade of his skin. And if the emissary was anything to judge by, some of them might be able to speak the Renian tongue as well as any Renian. He, on the other hand, was staring like a country eunuch, and had no one at his side who could speak Craitolian. His stomach twisted at the thought. He had no one he trusted to mediate for him, and the emissary was the only man whom he knew something of and could judge, and he seemed to be a man of many masks.

He swallowed his worry and forced a stern but indifferent expression upon his face as the two parties came to a halt across from each other. At a gesture from Chisin, the herald and standard bearer both stepped forward and announced his name, followed by the emissary's translation. There was a moment's silence that followed before the Qraul's herald announced him, and he stepped forward, a young man with a pinched face. No more than a boy, Gheyuth found himself thinking, before he remembered himself and sank to his knee, as Atasem had instructed him was proper for a dignitary at court.

He ducked his head in obeisance as well, which allowed him to hide his expression somewhat, for he was certain that his thoughts were written plainly there. He could not believe they were being led in this folly by a child, no matter that the stern-faced men standing behind him might be the ones holding the puppet strings. A child amidst the Adepts to face the Shadows.

•••

They had adjourned to the Qraul's tent, the interminable ceremonies finally completed, and none too soon with the heat of the day upon them. Keleprai and Byuvir, as the elder of the Gvers, had been asked to sit with the Qraul and the High Adept to discuss the coming battle with the Vazeir of Renuih. He had only one man accompanying him, called the Hjai Chisin. Keleprai was unsure whether that was his title or his name or both. Regardless, it was unpronounceable, like so many of the Renian names and honorifics. The other man with him, an Enir by his look, Keleprai now recognized as the High Adept's Disciple.

What masks we wear, he thought with a smile, recalling the song of that name, an insipid thing that had been popular two seasons ago. How had an Enir Adept been received in the land that had banned alkemya under penalty of death, he wondered, and guessed that it had been an uneasy thing at best. The Disciple's face hinted at none of the undercurrents that might reside there, but he had always been one to keep his robes folded close.

Within the tent, once everyone had been seated, there were further pleasantries and ceremonies, the elaborate politesse that hid the daggers in their sleeves. Laterala seemed to take great pleasure in these moments, the constant recitation of the same empty words, all to no end. It was the illusion of power, the only time when he was at the center of things.

When that was at last done, the Vazeir wasted little time in drawing to his point. "We are here as agreed, Most Immortal Qraul. The Most Gracious Ad Eselte requires that you make good the word that was given by your emissary with regard to silk trade."

These were the words the Disciple relayed to them after the Vazeir's blunt phrases. Keleprai cursed himself for not thinking to have Kigarle attend to him here. He knew the Renian tongue well enough to be able to say whether the Disciple was being honest in his translation. Cepedutherupt, he felt sure, could speak the imperial tongue. It was something he would be certain of before embarking on such a plan as he had, seeing this eventuality and not willing to leave such things to chance.

"Oh yes, naturally." Laterala nodded when the Disciple had finished his translation, though not, Keleprai noticed, without a glance at Cepedutherupt.

The High Adept had already motioned to one of the attendants, who brought forward the official treaty documents and set them in front of the Qraul, who placed his seal upon them with a flourish. The attendant passed them over to the Vazeir, who read them carefully before adding his signature and the Ad Eselte's seal. One copy he gave the Hjai Chisin, and the other he passed to the attendant, who bowed and exited the tent.

"Thank you and all praise to your magnificent Ad Eselte for joining us in this battle against our shared enemy. I hope that our triumph here and the ties that we are building with the silk trade will bring our two glorious realms closer together. Too long we have been cast apart."

Laterala finished with a flourish and smile, which Keleprai took to mean he had written the words he spoke himself.

The Vazeir appeared unimpressed as they were translated to him by the Disciple. "I shall pass on your kindness to our Most Immortal Ad Eselte. I am sure he shares in their sentiment. Now, Most Gracious Qraul of Craitol, I am afraid I must turn matters to what has brought us here. What are your plans here for the Shadows and the desert?"

An uncomfortable silence followed, Laterala unsure of himself, with the forms and protocols he was used to broken. He recovered a moment later and smiled. "Of course, Vazeir Gheyuth, we should not tarry in discussing strategy and logistics with the Shadows' harbor of darkness so near. I will let my advisors and you deal in the particulars, as they are better versed in these matters, as I'm sure are you. But we mean to root them from this place and destroy their stores of alkemya."

A look of distaste came over the Vazeir's face as the word *alkemya* was mentioned. He waited for the translation before saying, "We care nothing for alkemya. It is a scourge upon this realm nearly as great as the Shadows. But we are here because of them, and we will stand with you so long as you make no claim upon the desert. That city is ours, this place is ours, and it is to our eternal shame that we have yet to avenge our ancestors."

The silence that followed the Disciple's translation was longer and even more uncomfortable, and Keleprai had to resist a smile. There could be no doubt of the Disciple's translation, at least. When, he wondered, would Cepedutherupt step in and spare the boy any humiliation?

It was the High Adept who spoke next, his eyes hard. "The desert is of no concern to us. And you are correct—the alkemya in use here is a scourge and must be driven to ruin. We will do all that is necessary to see that happen."

The Vazeir stared at the High Adept as the Disciple translated what had been said. Keleprai watched them take the measure of each other, wondering what the Vazeir was thinking. Authority recognized authority, after all, and he would understand now who he would be dealing with in the days to come.

21

Eslyn...how often had he dreamed of this place, imagining wandering across its broken visage? Masiph wet his lips in excitement. And now to be here, with the wind carrying the scent of the desert to him, the afternoon sun heavy and bright, yet somehow distant in the vast sky above. Each step seemed momentous, his thoughts inadequate to what he was doing. There were no words for this triumph.

The stone laid out for its streets was still there, now broken in a multitude of places and overgrown with the scrub of the desert, and even trees in places. The presence of the trees and other vegetation indicated that the underground reservoirs which had drawn their ancestors to build here in the first place still provided. The skeletons of buildings remained in various states of completion, like the fossils one could find among the rocks in certain valleys by the Eresnan. The wall remained, though the breaches were numerous, whether from the Shadow Men invasion or the dereliction of time, Masiph could not say.

The wall was behind them now as his quadra headed north, deeper into the eastern half of the city. They had met the Craitolians at midday, just south of the ruins. After the ritual exchange of greetings and flags under the banners of the heralds, the Vazeir and the Hjai had gone within the Qraul of Craitol's tent to discuss the days to come. The two armies had idled, facing each other warily, under the full force of the midday sun, exposed to whatever Shadow Men forces lay in wait within the city.

They could see no one upon the walls, and the few scouts that each force sent to investigate returned to report that the streets were empty and the city deserted, by all appearances. When the Vazeir returned, he announced that they would be entering the city that day to lay claim to it and scour it of any Shadows. Masiph's quadra was one of three chosen for this sacred and glorious duty, which he knew amounted to little more than a scouting mission to see if any of the wells in the city were working and to see if there were in fact any Shadows there, as the Craitolians claimed.

"I am choosing you, Masiph den Ibrazil id Ezern," Gheyuth said to him, "because your family is of the desert. I am certain your father would appreciate the importance of this moment to your ancestors. See them honored today."

"Yes, Husem," Masiph said, lacking the words to say anything else, the moment overwhelming him with emotion.

The Craitolian took the city's western half, and Masiph led the Imperial Army into the eastern side. The men were quiet at first; Masiph could feel their nervousness as well as his own, no one trusting the word of the advance scouts, knowing the Shadows could be lurking around any corner. But as they went further, the other two quadras separating off to explore other byways of the city, they all began to relax as it became clear the city had been abandoned. All that remained of the Shadows were the rings of their tents and fires, along with some broken pottery and implements. The detritus of a people, which the wind would soon wash away.

The men began to argue with one another as to why the Shadow Men had left the city. Yuluir declared loudly, as if daring the others to disagree, that the Shadows could not stomach a fair match. They would only attack if they had a clear numerical advantage or, as in the case of their raids, if they had surprise on their side.

"A sensible strategy," Nustef said with authority. Masiph smiled to hear it. His friend was still recovering from the flux, his breath still heavy in his chest and his step still unsure, but his eyes had cleared and his smile had returned.

"It is the kerchief Erise gave me," he had told Masiph after being released from the quarantine. "It has brought me luck and the blessing of my ancestors."

Masiph looked at it now, tied about his friend's throat, a

gleaming blue, and had to resist a smile of joy. He could not imagine the despair he would have felt if he had lost his friend, had been the cause of his death, bringing him along on what to this point had been a terrible adventure. Triumph now lay around the corner, he was certain. Their ancestors would see them both blessed.

"A strategy of cowards," Yuluir said with a sneer. "These vermin run from us, and nothing more. They'll never stand and fight, and you know it. They haven't the appetite for anything but abuse amongst their fellows. I would never bring shame on my ancestors by doing such a thing."

"No you wouldn't," Nustef said in a tone of dismissal.

Yuluir halted and stepped into the second's path. "You think I wear the hood? Will you follow your mouth with your sword?"

"The hood is over your eyes," Nustef said. "Take a moment to think before speaking. Would you defend this city?"

Yuluir did not reply, and Nustef nodded. "Exactly. They had no time to rebuild the walls. They had no idea we were coming, at least not until it was too late to do anything. So why stand and fight here, defending the indefensible? Better to draw us back out into the hills, where they would be able to find an advantage."

"Do you think that's where they are?" someone else asked him.

"That's where I would be. Or maybe they have fled. It's hard to say how many of them were living here."

Even Yuluir could see the sense in his words, and the argument was ended. Since the awful night when they had been forced to stand with Gheyuth as he put down the revolt of their fellow sulihers, the men had shown far more respect for Nustef and Masiph. Although they had all been reluctant to kill their fellow men, they had followed the orders they had been given, and Masiph now felt himself truly their jetthir. Strangely, the other quadras, and their jetthirs, all kept their distance from them, as if they were now members of the Vazeir's personal guard. Masiph had heard mutterings that they were now familiars of the emissary, just as his father was. He could only hope that once the interminable waiting was over and the fighting had begun in earnest, this would all be forgotten.

They continued on down the empty streets, breaking off in groups of two or three to investigate this or that structure to see if there was anything of value that had been left behind. The area they were in had seemingly been a merchant district, for the buildings that remained standing were mostly courtyard houses of two or three stories, not large enough for a Nohritai of substance, but a place that would declare to those passing by that the owner was not without means.

The street they were on came to an end, along with two others, at a crumbling edifice, once a public building of some sort. There were three wings coming off the main structure, which housed a courtyard, only one of which remained standing. A short wall, hardly rising above any of their chests, still stood, its edges worn by the wind. Nustef sent half the men in to explore while the rest idled outside.

A shout from within put them all on edge, everyone grasping their spears tighter and raising up their shields, as though expecting the Shadows to simply materialize before them.

"They are not Adepts," Masiph said when no further cries came, and there were a few bitter laughs.

Duhalleh emerged from within the ruin to say they had found s working well. He led them back, the rest of the quadra following, through the inner courtyard and the main building to the only standing wing. It had a large garden at its end, enclosed by the other wings and a wall, a few weary fruit trees all that remained of its splendor. The well was in their midst, a recent addition by its look, and a couple of the men had already begun to push at its wheel.

They cheered when the water spilled down the funnel to ground. A couple of them leaned in to sniff at it, but all they could smell was the cool earth below. Nustef stepped forward and cupped a few handfuls into his mouth and then washed his face. They all watched him, the men who had been pushing at wheel stopping as well.

He shrugged. "It's fine, I think. Hard to poison, at any rate, if it is connected to the aquifer."

That was enough reassurance for them all. They filled their canteens and then hurried out of the place.

"We'll be lucky to make it back before dark," Masiph said to Nustef, glancing up at the sun which growing low in the sky. They had perhaps an hour's worth of light left.

Nustef did not reply and Masiph turned to him and saw that he had come to an abrupt halt at the entrance. Masiph stopped as well, confused for a moment. His confusion ended as he followed Nustef's gaze and saw the horde of Shadow Men moving down one of the side streets toward them.

•••

Vyissan sat across from Cepedutherupt, Disciple to Adept, for the first time in weeks, though it felt like it had been years. So much had happened in the intervening days, yet the High Adept looked unchanged, his careful, serene expression still in place, his watchful eyes studying Vyissan. What did they see, he wondered? He had offered no comment when Vyissan had brought Phariayh into the vast Qraul's tent. That would come, though, Vyissan knew, but for now, other matters pressed him.

"What can you tell me of this Vazeir?" Cepedutherupt said.

They had also not discussed the two days—or was it three?—when Vyissan had not responded to any of the High Adept's entreaties, a violation of the bond between Adept and Disciple. Vyissan had prepared his excuses, though he was not sure any of them would withstand the High Adept's scrutiny.

"He is faithful to the Empire above all else. So long as he sees our interests aligning, he will observe the alliance, but he will not stand if we find ourselves in a great deal of trouble. He is no fool. And he believes absolutely in the prohibition against alkemya."

Cepedutherupt gave him a wry smile. "An interesting journey for you, then."

"It was not easy."

"No. And the hardest work remains."

Vyissan nodded. He did not want to think of that, though it had never been far from his thoughts these last days.

An attendant arrived to replenish their water and announce that dinner would be served in half an hour, and the Qraul was expecting their presence. Cepedutherupt thanked the man and turned back to Vyissan. "If the Shadows truly have abandoned the city, they will have taken the engines with them and we will have to follow. Will the Vazeir join us in such a venture?"

Vyissan shook his head. "I think not, unless we can somehow convince him that his interest lies there. They want this city, and if they cannot hold it they will return to Renuih."

"What if we threaten to break the treaty and end the silk trade?"

"He stands to make no coin over it, I think," Vyissan said. "And I don't believe he thinks highly of the Imperial Vazeir or the Ad Eselte for allying with us."

"Because of the alkemya."

"Yes. He understands it, of course, and accepts it and will see the Ad Eselte's designs carried out as far as it goes."

"And this," Cepedutherupt said, gesturing toward the unseen ruins that lay beyond the tent, "is as far as that is."

Vyissan nodded, and Cepedutherupt ran a worried hand through his hair. "If only we had not been delayed."

"That is the other thing," Vyissan said. "They lost a third of their men, at least. Maybe as many as half or two-thirds fell ill. They are weak, and he will not press them if he thinks they will be broken. Too many of their ancestors lost their way in the desert."

Cepedutherupt looked pensive and unsure of himself, something Vyissan had only rarely seen in his Adept. "I must give blood to Melinon so we might see the way."

Before he could rise, an alarm went up in both camps, and moments later a runner arrived from the wall. Laterala came into their chamber after the message had been delivered, his face pale and his hand trembling.

"The Shadows are in the city," he said.

22

"They've left us for dead. They've left us for dead. Carrion for the beasts. By the Gods, they have."

The boy was muttering to himself like he was under a fever. Donier glanced at him from the corner of his eye for only a moment before returning his gaze to the empty streets below. The morning's shadows were still long in the open doorways, the sun crawling up the horizon behind them after another harrowing night. The day would bring no relief.

"They know. They'll just sit there and starve us out and then collect their plunder. They know."

There was more as Ehedien went into graphic detail as to the nature of their fate at the hands of the Shadows. Something about the Shadow Men leaving their starved and broken bodies to their familiars, the vultures and tolotes, once they were through ransacking their flesh. Donier ignored him. If there were Shadow Men out there, they were staying out of sight and out of bow range. He frowned and rubbed his jaw, trying not to think of just how much he wanted the taste of a quid in his mouth. The taste of anything, really.

He and the boy had been on watch near the mausoleum gate since just before sunrise, trying to divine shapes out of the darkness. Not that he expected an attack. After yesterday, the Shadows had no illusions as to the strength of their numbers, as they had sought to storm various points of the wall throughout the day to no avail. There was no need to force the situation when they had to know as well that the food and water within these walls was limited. It was only a matter of waiting, especially if, as appeared to be the case, the rest of the army was suffering under similar circumstances.

That was the worst, actually, not knowing what was happening beyond these walls. That no pigeons had arrived with news or instructions in the two days since the Shadow Men had emerged from somewhere within the city seemed to spell doom. All they could do was wait and pray to the Gods.

"They've left us for dead," Ehedien said, repeating it like a litany.

"Be quiet and have some mettle," he told the boy. "Or is your brain so sodden from the camp kettles you are bereft of reason?"

"And what of them? Spoils for the Shadows, no doubt. Cracked beyond repair."

"They're fine. There's not an honest thrust among the Shadow Men."

"Not honest in combat, either. They wait until they have us at all fours and then fall upon us."

"They haven't yet," Donier said.

"No. They are teasing us, like any cat of the mountain."

Donier sighed, wanting very much to hit him. *Just a boy*, he told himself, *and he's terrified*. Who wouldn't be?

"We are not abandoned. They would've overwhelmed us by now if that were the case. You saw how many there were out there, and you can probably double that. Like rats. If the Qraul had been chased off, or, Gods forbid, killed, then the Shadows would be coming at us until they had us all killed. But they wait."

The boy was silent, thinking about what had been said. Donier hoped it was convincing enough; he couldn't take much more of his talk. He was spared it by the arrival of a pigeon flying in high overhead, its wings catching the light from the still emerging sun. Someone inside the wall spotted it and yelled for the handler, who called it down. He craned his neck up, trying to pick it out of the sky, but he was facing into the sun so he couldn't make anything out. From the cheers that rose around behind them, he knew that it had come down. Something quivered inside him, and he feared he might weep.

"You see," he said to Ehedien, as casually as he could, "we are not abandoned."

When he was done at the wall, Donier wandered back to where his cohort was camped near the entrance to the mausoleum complex. Most of the men—there were nearly one hundred who had managed to retreat to this stronghold—had situated themselves in the open area between the mausoleum and the gate. There was a long walkway from the gate to the necropolis entrance, shaded at odd intervals by four trees, one of which was dead and hollow. That had been cut down almost immediately for firewood, while the other three were being slowly stripped of their meager bark and leaves as the soldiers sought out anything in the compound that might so much as resemble food.

Ludenn had placed him in charge of the cohort. There were parts of four cohorts that had gathered here, but he had been the only kehel to survive, or at least to make it within the walls. Donier was one of three seconds, each of whom had been placed in charge of a cohort of thirty or so. They had divided the days in thirds, morning to midday, midday to midnight, and midnight to morning, with one cohort standing watch at all times. Straws had been drawn, and Donier's men had received the morning-to-midday watch.

Yesterday had been the first day of this routine, one punctuated throughout by the Shadow Men probing for weaknesses in their defenses. Only a few men had been killed, and two others looked as though they had wounds that would lead them to perish. Today looked to be calmer, if no less harrowing, the moments where nothing interceded only allowing them to reflect on the uncomfortable reality of their situation.

Most of the cohort was lying on the ground and staring off into the half-distance, no doubt trying not to think about the food they could not eat. There were a few going over their weapons, sharpening blades and points, cleaning pommels and the like, seeking refuge in that monotony past coherence, rather than thinking of the oblivion that faced them. He wandered among them, giving them what words of encouragement he could summon.

As he was making his rounds, a soldier from another cohort approached and said, "Nes Donier? Nes Ludenn asks for you."

He thanked the man and made his way to the mausoleum where the Ludenn had established his command. Each step nearer his destination only deepened his trepidation. It was the oddest thing. As soon as the cheers had subsided at the sight of the pigeon, he had been crushed by an overwhelming sense of doom, which was only worsened by the necessity of putting up a strong front before Ehedien on the wall. Once his shift had been over he should have gone immediately to Ludenn, but he hadn't—he had sought instead to avoid the meeting. He did not want to know what the note the pigeon had carried said.

If anything, they had been lucky to this point, his cohort especially. When the Shadows had pulled tight their snare, appearing from nowhere in the midst of those cohorts that had been sent into the ruined city, theirs had somehow slipped the loop that the Shadow Men had snapped tight on the others. By chance they had passed the mausoleum moments earlier, and it seemed the obvious place to fall back to. They had retreated behind the walls, suffering only minimal losses, fortunate again, for the numbers opposite them were small.

They spent a terrifying, exhausting night fending off the Shadows along the walls while they also sought to seal up the wall's entrance with whatever large stones they could manage to drag from the mausoleum. The Gods had smiled on them in this as well, for the entrance was slim—three men could fill the gap—and so it was both easy to defend and easy to fill with whatever rubble they could find. The walls were about seven feet tall, with defenses that mimicked those of a city wall or palace. Once darkness fell they had lit torches to help guide their work at fortification, hoping as well to signal to the other cohorts trapped in the city.

Remnants of three other cohorts had fled to the wall throughout the night and into the next morning, forcing them to send men beyond the wall to help bring them within. The majority though had come at once, close to dawn. They had been trapped together in the ambush, and had kept their formation and battled their way to the mausoleum throughout the night. Their arrival had brought their numbers to nearly one hundred, a blessing and a curse, for it meant there would be no trouble holding the mausoleum against great force, but what meager food and fuel there was would be exhausted all the more quickly.

For most of that night and the next day, the Shadows had not outnumbered them significantly, and their attacks had focused solely on the gate. Yesterday, truly terrifying numbers had come in wave upon wave, emerging from some unseen place in the streets beyond, so near the men barely had time to let loose a barrage of arrows before they were at the walls and throwing up their ladders. So far those at the wall had held strong; not one Shadow had set foot upon the ramparts, and their dead were strewn on the ground below.

And now they were left with a stalemate, if a temporary one. The cost was too great for the Shadow Men to try to storm the wall, especially when one considered that all they need do was wait. All those within the walls could hope for was that whatever remained of the army beyond the city was together and fighting.

Donier had not slept since the attack, though he had tried yesterday after his time at the wall. He had lain for what must have been an hour, but which had felt like four or five, unable to stop his mind from going down the very paths he had chided Ehedien for this morning. There was a weight behind his eyes that ached with a dull persistence. The daylight seemed washed out of color, empty of the sharpness that he was used to.

He nearly stumbled on the steps up into the mausoleum. The building itself was large, the size of a small estate house, but there was only one room within. Empty now that they had taken every loose piece of stone or statuary that had still remained. The dome above was open at its center, illuminating the room below. There were levels below this one of the men had told him, but he had not bothered to venture down there yet.

Ludenn was stretched out near the door, his eyes closed. He sat up when he heard Donier enter.

"Anything on the wall?" he asked, blinking as he took in who was before him.

Donier shook his head. "No, they're sitting back. Waiting."

Ludenn cleared his throat and spat out into the surrounding dimness. "You saw there was a message."

Donier grunted and sat down across from him, enjoying the cool of the stone beneath him. Neither of them spoke, and Donier let his eyes close.

"They aren't coming for us," Ludenn said at last.

"No."

"No. Gods curse them. They want us to stay here. We're drawing a lot of the Shadows, apparently. At least, they think so. It will let them do something else."

"What? Retreat?"

Ludenn ignored that. "We'll have to try to improve the defenses, I think. I'd like trenches in front of the walls. I'm going to assign your cohort to that. If they are not going to attack, we need to use that time. I think you should cut down one of the trees for spears."

"It won't be enough."

"Then cut down all of them, if that's what you need," Ludenn said, his voice echoing throughout the room.

Donier opened one eye to look at his kehel. "Do they know our situation?"

"Yes. Gods curse them. This was a reply to our bird." Ludenn looked away, back toward the fraying circle of light extending down from the ceiling. There were carvings there of whatever triumphs the dead lying below had achieved Gods knew how many centuries before.

"Once you get the trench work done, we'll be better defended. We can spare a force to go out into the city to see if we can find some food and water."

"They'll just get themselves killed," Donier said.

Ludenn shrugged. *What did it matter?*

23

Phariayh moved restlessly about the room of the tent the emissary had brought her to when the armies had met and he had rejoined his people. He had said he would be some time, as he had to translate for the Vazeir of the Imperial Army while he spoke to the Ad Eselte of Craitol about the coming battle, and there might be other ceremonies to follow, but he would be back in the evening to make sure she had settled into these new quarters. And to take his pleasure, no doubt, but he had not spoken of that. He had promised to teach her something of his tongue and to ensure she had a place among his people, all vague oaths, easily forgotten and set aside.

That had been two days ago, and she had not seen him since. The Shadows attacked that evening; Phariayh had heard the alarms followed by the marshaling of the various forces. She left the tent and stood with the other attendants to watch as the sulihers and their jetthirs assembled before marching into the city. The emissary and a group of other men gathered outside moments later, and followed the armies forward to the city wall. The emissary caught sight of her as he passed by, their eyes locking briefly, his expression blank and guarded, before turning his attention back to the man at his side.

As she watched his figure dwindle into the distance, she became aware of the stares of the attendants beside her. When she turned to look at them, one of them stepped forward, a eunuch by the look of him, and spat on the ground before her, making a warding sign with his hands. Several others made gestures as well that she did not recognize, one saying something in the Craitolian tongue.

She did not need to know the words and gestures to understand their intent, and she shivered as a tendril of fear crept through her. She felt exposed standing there alone in the midst of all these red-shaded foreigners, feeling the difference of her shade all the more, and she scurried back inside to the room Atasem had brought her to. There she stayed for the rest of the night, waiting for the emissary to return, even as she wondered why, until at last she fell asleep on the ground beside his bed.

Hunger drove her from her room the next morning when she awoke, well before dawn, and she stole from the tent and found the wagons and tents nearby where the attendants kept their supplies and prepared the meals for the Ad Eselte of Craitol. No one was awake, and she stole some ardeh cheese and milk, as well as half a loaf of a strange, dark bread. She ate it all throughout the day, not leaving the tent chamber. At some point she gave up waiting for the emissary to return, and slept upon his bed, thinking that she should enjoy such luxuries while they were hers to take, for such things, she knew, never lasted.

Now it was nearly morning again, and the emissary still had not returned. Her hunger had, though, and she knew she would have to leave again to see if she could steal some more food. The longer she remained in the Craitolian camp without the emissary as her protector, the more precarious her position felt. At least with the Renians she could speak the tongue and make herself understood, which was a comfort, however small. At least she might be able to find out what was going on. Right now she had no way of knowing when the emissary would return, or indeed if.

That alone was reason enough to risk leaving her chambers and the tent to see what remained of the camp, and so she quit pacing and slipped out of the tent, emerging to the first light of dawn, the sun just touching the horizon. The camp seemed largely empty, but for the attendants, sutlers and camp followers. The armies remained somewhere beyond the wall in the ruined city, but for a few quadras.

She could see sentries on watch at the edges of the camps, and an area where the wounded were being kept. The breeze shifted as she stood there, and the stench of putrefaction touched her nostrils and she realized they were not all wounded lying there. The thought made her shudder—if they did not have time to bury their dead, how badly might things be going? She thought of the emissary telling her that he would be entering the cauldron and would be unlikely to survive. Perhaps they all were in the cauldron he had spoken of, about to be engulfed.

If that were the case, Phariayh decided, she needed to seize whatever she could now, while time remained. She retraced her steps to the supply wagon, but saw that some of the attendants were already up and busy preparing breakfast and warming themselves by the fire. One of them caught sight of her lingering hopefully and shouted something, throwing his cup of dala at her. She dodged out of the way and moved back, going further as the man bluffed chasing after her.

She returned to the tent, hesitating at the threshold. What use was there remaining here if the emissary was not to be her protector? If the war went badly, as seemed to be the case, these people were as likely to turn on her as the Renians, perhaps more so. There was nowhere here for her, no place in all the realms. She started away from the camp, heading into the desert.

•••

Masiph sat coiled in a ball, his arms clenched tight around his knees, upon which he rested on his chin. He shifted his gaze between the doorway and where Nustef lay, still for the moment, his shallow breathing stirred from time to time by formless mutters. Masiph watched the slow rise and fall of his friend's chest, trying to find some sign of recovery in them. It was a futile effort, so he closed his eyes instead, but that only sharpened his ears to the chattering of the Shadows below.

They were in the garden around the well, the water spilling down the trough to their buckets and canteens as they talked. It was agonizing to listen to their talk in that guttural tongue he did not understand. In his mind, every one of them was wondering about the strange noise coming from the ruins above them. He could only hope by the grace of his ancestors that Nustef remained quiet.

There was a window in the next room that overlooked the garden. The previous night, his third trapped within the ruins, he had summoned what remained of his courage and gone to peer down at the gardens to see if the Shadows left them uninhabited. The courtyard appeared empty, and so tonight he planned to head below to the well. He could wait no longer. Both canteens had been empty since morning, and his throat ached from the dry desert heat.

The clatter of the pump halted, and the sound of the Shadows' talk slowly diminished. He waited until it had been quiet for at least a minute before he stretched out his legs and stood. He sighed in relief as he walked around the room, working the stiffness from his knee. It was much better than it had been yesterday. If he encountered someone tonight, he thought he might be able to move fast enough to escape.

He limped over to Nustef and crouched beside him, checking the dressing covering the wound in his chest. He had put it on that morning, but it was already wet with blood at midday. Changing it offered a welcome distraction, and he tore up some more of his outer robe and then lifted Nustef up into a seated pose, kneeling behind him to prop him up as he took off the dressing and cleaned the wound. The arrow had passed cleanly through his chest, and both ends wept with blood and a clear liquid, which he took to be a sign that there was no infection.

When he finished reapplying the dressing, Masiph set his friend down carefully and returned to his agonized pacing, the Shadow Men never far from his thoughts. When he closed his eyes he would see them swarming toward the quadra, cutting down everyone within reach with the rest of the sulihers scattering across the grounds. Somehow he had danced through that scythe, escaping their initial assault and making it back to the ruined building.

Nustef was a step behind him, almost to safety, when he took an arrow to the chest, near his heart. Masiph heard his cry, and turned to see him lying in the open just beyond the door's threshold. He turned and darted out into the open, seizing Nustef by the shoulders and dragging him within the building. As he did so, he saw a Shadow bludgeon Yuluir with his own shield, breaking off the top part of his skull and sending the contents within spilling out.

Masiph did not linger in the doorway to see more, following some others as they fled down various hallways, dragging Nustef with him. He paused for a moment to gather his bearings, and lifted Nustef over his shoulder before heading into one of the collapsed wings, hoping it might dissuade the Shadows from following. He came to a broken stairway and scrambled up it, twisting his knee in the process, and then navigated a path through the rubble that lay above. He dragged Nustef, an arrow still protruding from his chest, over stone and wood, heedless of whatever damage he might be causing. At one juncture the building was caved in and he was forced to shove the rubble aside to create a path, cutting his hands and arms in the frenzied process.

After that, he came to an area where the roof and walls had fallen away, leaving an exposed walkway. On its other side there was a section of the wing that appeared whole. The exposure faced out into the garden where the well lay, and from his vantage point he watched the remainder of his quadra being killed. When the Shadows had completed their business and left, he limped as fast as his leg and Nustef's weight would allow him across what seemed a vast expanse. The second moaned loudly as he did so, and Masiph winced, hoping against hope that whatever Shadow Men were in the vicinity were too far away to hear it.

There were only the two rooms beside one another where the roof, floor and walls were all more or less intact, and he chose the one without the window as their hiding place. He stayed crouched by the doorway clutching his sword, listening to the Shadows below as they returned to deal with the bodies, obviously having killed any of the sulihers who had managed to escape. He waited at least an hour after the final sound of their passage had gone before he relaxed his guard and tended to Nustef's wound, his hands shaking.

After, he had waited, hoping for his ancestors to reveal something to him. Some manner of escape from this crumbling sanctuary which now imprisoned him, some method of healing Nustef, who he knew was grievously wounded, or some means of letting the rest of the army know that he was still alive and within Esyln. None presented themselves and so he continued waiting, wondering if all was already lost and the army fled back to Renuih.

Masiph was still pacing and waiting that day when the Shadow Men returned for more water. They left before the sunset, and he waited until well after darkness had settled across the ruined city, the wind gone still, the birds quiet, before he dared to leave the room and stray across the open expanse that lay between him and the rest of the building. It was even longer before he found his way through wreckage to the main entrance. When he emerged there was blood on his face and arms, and his knee was so sore he could barely put weight on it.

In spite of that, he forced himself to investigate the entire grounds to ensure there were no stray Shadows on watch. There was a half-moon above to guide him, making his task somewhat easier. There was no sign of any Shadows, nor could see any evidence of what had become of his men. He had heard the Shadows left the bodies of their dead for the tolotes, and he had hoped somehow to spare his quadra that fate. It was not to be, though, and he could only hope that their ancestors would find their spirits and that his own would not curse him for this failure.

When he had completed his circuit of the grounds, he returned to the gardens and went to the well. The pump groaned as he started to push it, and he ducked below the well's lip, feeling foolish as he did so. He stood slowly, looking around, but his only companions were the trees and stars. The pump seemed to make an extraordinary amount of noise as he pushed it, and he was certain it could be heard blocks away, but he kept at it anyway, filling both canteens and drinking his fill.

Before he left the enclosure, he walked over to the fruit trees and filled his robe with some apples and plums. The oranges he left for they were mostly rotten and the birds had been at them. He returned above to where Nustef waited on the dagger's edge of life, but Masiph was smiling as he went, a crazed ecstasy seizing him. He had water and food now, and he knew he could get more, and if fortune and his ancestors smiled on him again, he would be ready.

•••

Where the wind has washed the rocks clean. That was the phrase that had nearly driven Vyissan mad these last days as he and the High Adept had pored over the maps given him by the Ad Eselte and tried to discern some key or hidden codex that might illuminate the entrance to the labyrinth that lay beneath the city's ruined visage. The two maps of the city proper gave no indication that a maze lay underneath the carefully delineated streets, while the map of the labyrinth showed only the path through to the administrator's palace, the location of the entrance marked only by that phrase.

Lining up the maps against each other gave them a general sense of where they needed to be looking: somewhere in the vicinity of their camp. The problem was that, in all likelihood, those words had been rendered meaningless by the intervening decades, the rocks either gone or altered beyond recognition. It seemed as good a strategy to ignore the phrase and look for its opposite, though what that might be, he could not say.

Cepedutherupt had tasked he and several Enir mercenaries to the search, which they had begun in the aftermath of the Shadows' ambush within Esyln and continued for the last two days almost without respite. Vyissan could barely stand now, hardly see, yet the High Adept, seemingly inexhaustible, continued to peer at the maps and send him forth with another group of mercenaries to go over the hard desert ground. He had managed an hour's worth of sleep the night before, lying at Cepedutherupt's feet as the High Adept muttered over the maps, too tired to even find his way through the Qraul's tent to his quarters, where Phariayh awaited him.

The ground south of the city wall, where the map seemed to suggest the entrance lay, was full of rock, jagged and broken, barren of all but a few cacti that seemed to thrive on the more unforgiving earth. The barren terrain was flat as well, so no matter where he went he could still see to the camp and the walls beyond, out to the hills that rose up all around the north and east of the city. He watched as the wounded were carried out from within the walls back to curing tents, numbers beyond measuring, it seemed, and knew that their time to find the entrance was short.

Now the train of wounded had stopped with night upon them and the battles in the city ceasing for the moment. The itch of alkemya, the working of the astral, the casting of the germ, and the thrust and parry of alkemy, had subsided as well. Almost from the moment their forces had been ambushed in Esyln, the Shadows had turned the engines upon the Council Adepts. For the moment they held firm, but even with Vyissan and Cepedutherupt to stand with them, they could not hope to overwhelm the Shadows. They had too many engines, producing too much alkemya.

"There is nothing to obscure the view out there," he told Cepedutherupt. They were some distance from the Qraul's tent, the shroud of darkness heavy on them and above Senteur's heavens.

"They would not take an escape tunnel out to the hills. It is there somewhere."

Vyissan nodded. "It has to be, but whatever was there that hid it is gone. And maybe it is too. Perhaps the Shadows closed it off."

"Perhaps."

They were obviously familiar with the labyrinth, having used it to secrete their forces when the armies had entered the city. If they were aware of the labyrinth, it was reasonable to assume they were aware of its entrance beyond the city. Why, then, had they not used it to attack them from behind, or possible even within, their camp? It was not as though they lacked for numbers, if the reports from within the city were true. It made no sense to Vyissan, unless they had sealed the entrance, fearing that an attacking army would do exactly what the High Adept intended, launch an attack at the heart of their alkemyc engines.

"We do not have time to look for it," the High Adept said with exasperation. "We have to find it now. I can keep our forces inside the walls, and the Enir companies too, but the Renians will leave. If they do, we won't be able to hold. We have to find it."

Vyissan did not reply; there was nothing to say. They had been over the ground in darkness and in light and it had all revealed nothing. He thought of the days, weeks even, it might take if they had to expand the search farther, even into the hills. But that was time they did not have. It all left him more exhausted then he already was.

The night seemed to swim around him, his vision blurring with exhaustion, and he had to catch himself from drifting off where he stood. Cepedutherupt was watching him, and he said, "Go to bed. We both should. There is nothing left to do tonight. We will talk in the morning and see if sleep brings anything to light."

Vyissan nodded, and they both turned back to the Qraul's tent. Cepedutherupt, he knew, would not be going to sleep. The High Adept would pore over the maps until morning, give more blood to Melinon, and send Vyissan out on what would likely be another futile search over the same terrain. The thought nearly made him weep, but, he told himself, it was a problem for tomorrow. Tonight he would set such thoughts and problems aside and sleep with Phariayh in his arms. He only hoped the last days had not been trying for her. The thought was a comfort to him until, after several confused false turns, he made his way through the tent and back to his quarters and saw that Phariayh was gone.

24

Hunger was like its own creature within him, sometimes loud in anguish, often dull and stupid, and in rare moments silent. But the presence never left. Donier had a little food and water left in his supply, but the dribs and drabs he allowed himself only served to make his appetite all the more fearsome. The morning they had entered the city, each man had been given two days' rations and water, in the event something like this disaster took place. Donier had supervised the distribution, granting himself second's preference and taking some extra food. Now, four days later, supplies had grown precarious.

It had been noticeably cooler the last two days though, a reprieve of sorts. If nothing else it made the trench work he had led the day before less of a burden. The Shadows, except for a few bow shots that fell short, mostly left them to the task. Ludenn sent the first expedition out in search of water on the second morning, twelve men only.

"It will have to be enough," Ludenn said, and Donier thought it almost certainly would not be, but said nothing. Twelve fewer men to starve with was all it meant. If those on the expedition had any sense, they would run and hope the Shadows were too preoccupied to bother with them. Treasonous thoughts, surely.

"There's another stair here," Ehedien whispered to him, peering back through the shadows from where he crouched. To distract himself from his hunger and the boy from his increasingly mad thoughts, Donier had proposed an expedition of their own to explore what lay beneath the mausoleum.

"Solid?" he asked as he went over to crouch beside the boy. Ehedien nodded. Several of the men had ventured down to the level immediately below the great room where Ludenn had set up his command, but none, so far as he knew, had gone any farther. They were now three levels down into the tombs, and faced with a fourth. Donier led the way, holding the torch high as he gingerly tested the steps.

"It's all the same," Ehedien said, disappointed when they reached the bottom.

Donier had to agree, though he remained fascinated by all that he saw. How far down did it go, he wondered? There had to be generations entombed here, abandoned to the vicissitudes of the desert and the Shadow Men. They stood in an open chamber, low-ceilinged with thick cobwebs hanging in their faces. There was a smell, not of death exactly, more the staleness of inertia.

It seemed clear from the stairways, and the surprisingly broad corridors that had branched off this chamber, that these passages had been well used, which made sense, he supposed. They would have been making offerings or burying the newly dead, presumably. And it explained the weirdness of the place, the fact that none of the stone and earthen stairs or walls had begun to crumble or collapse. If he were to guess, he would say that, excepting the cobwebs and the sourness of the air, it was much as the Renians had left it when they abandoned the city.

Donier went a few steps down the corridor on his left, casting his torch from side to side. He stopped at one of the tombs, this one sealed in wood rather than the stone that had been used on the others. Some insects had eaten away at the one corner, and when he pulled at the wood there it broke away in chunks. He cleared an opening large enough for him to stick his head and the torch through. He had no idea what he might find behind the wall, aside from the body he presumed would be there. What else one might put in a tomb, he did not know.

The entire concept was, if not quite blasphemous, against the intentions of the Gods, though he was unclear on the exact theological points. A spirit needed to be free and purified of the encumbrance of the flesh in order to find its way to Ulternon's Hall, should it be so blessed. They were committing blasphemy right now with their dead lying beyond the walls along with the bodies of the Shadow Men. They had no wood to spare to burn them, no cureder to do the proper invocations.

The tomb was not anything like he had expected. For one, there was no body, at least that he could see. There was nothing at all in sight but further darkness stretching out beyond the illumination of his torch. Donier had assumed that all the tombs were small chambers carved out of the corridors where the bodies were placed and then sealed over, but this suggested that there were further tunnels, and who knew what else beyond.

"What is it like?" Ehedien whispered from behind him.

"Not really sure," Donier replied, easing his way out of the opening and stepping back to allow the boy a look.

"It's a tunnel."

"So it appears."

"Are they all like this?"

"One wonders."

Ehedien jerked his head out with a sudden movement, nearly striking it on the door as he did. He looked at Donier as though he were about to ask him a question, before thrusting himself back through the hole, this time holding his torch behind him.

When at last he removed his head again, he turned to Donier. "I think I feel a draft."

Donier looked at him, a tremor of feeling coursing through him. He followed the boy's example, putting his head in the opening, the torch outside, peering into the unchanging darkness. He waited, hearing his stomach groan. And then there it was, the barest hint, but there all the same, a touch of air to his face that was cool and sweet. There and gone.

The sun was obscured behind the hills to the east as they set out, the light still dim enough that they could convince themselves they were not exposed as they walked openly down the streets. Even so, they stayed in an instinctive crouch as they walked, ready to flee at a moment's notice. Donier tugged at his robes uncomfortably, his back already soaked with sweat, though the morning was cool. There were six men with him. He had asked for twice that, and been told by Ludenn this was all that could be spared.

"You will have a better odds with fewer men," Ludenn said. "Less likely to attract the notice of the Shadows."

Donier doubted that very much—the odds were not in their favor no matter how many men they sent—but he had not said anything. The first men who had been sent out two days before had been volunteers, preferring the risk of whatever awaited them in the ruined city to the slow torture of waiting within the mausoleum for their own deaths. Their failure to return had meant that only half a dozen men stepped forward when Ludenn had asked the night before.

Donier had said he would lead the force; he could no longer stand to wait for the end to come. Five days now, strains of madness seeping into all of them. There was no food left, or nothing worth mentioning. The condensation traps they had set up had worked better than he had expected, given how dry the air was, but they could not even hope to get enough water to meet their needs. Men had started passing out on the walls. Another pigeon had arrived from the army, asking them to hold out a few days more.

"We have been sacrificed," he said to Ludenn when the kehel came to see them off.

Ludenn ignored him, looking to the carrier standing beside him with the pigeon perched upon his arm. "Just find water. Even if you can't get any back. So long as we know where a well is."

They were past the first line of buildings across the street from the mausoleum, halfway down the street. The group that had gone out the day before had made it this far, had in fact disappeared from the sight of those manning the wall. And that was the last they had been seen or heard from. Within the walls of the mausoleum, they were not sure what this meant. Did it mean that the Shadows were being pressed elsewhere and could not afford the forces to maintain the siege? Or were they simply content to sit back and wait, knowing there was nothing in the buildings and streets surrounding the mausoleum that those trapped within could use?

Another group was set to follow them to investigate the immediate vicinity to see if there was anything of value they could lay their hands on. No one had high hopes. Their faith rested with Donier's men, who were to go as far into the city as they could, as far they could make it beyond whatever barricades or lines the Shadow Men had established. There had to be wells. Judging by the number of waterworks they had passed on various streets to get here, water supply had not been a concern in Esyln. It was just a matter of finding them, and how well guarded they might be.

At the end of the street, Donier changed directions, heading north, away from wherever the Craitolian army might be holding ground, assuming they still did, and hopefully where fewer Shadows could be found. They continued moving out of sight of the walls, past any hope of a safe retreat. He tried to look everywhere at once, to peer into the shadowed gloom of collapsed doorways, to see what was lurking around distant corners, if the glint in the distance was a blade catching the arriving dawn or just an illusion created by the rising sun.

They crossed one street and then another. Two blocks and no sign of the Shadow Men. He found himself relaxing slightly, the muscles in his shoulders and back loosening, though he knew the fact they had encountered no one only increased the chances encountering someone on the streets ahead. These were not odds to play. There were any number of explanations for the Shadows' absence, all tantalizingly reasonable, all sure to be false.

They did not see them until after the attack had already begun. One of the men beside Donier fell with an arrow in his chest just as another sailed past his head. He glanced back in time to see another barrage of arrows launched from behind one of the buildings they had just passed, and he managed to get his shield up before they arrived. One of the projectiles notched itself in the leather. Some of the other men were not as lucky—he saw two others who caught arrows, including the carrier, and someone else was screaming in agony. From the corner of his eye he saw a half-dozen Shadows materialize from behind the rubble-strewn remains directly across from where he was crouched.

Donier did not wait. He was on his feet and running as fast as he could manage. He dodged as he went, cutting between buildings and down alleys, never keeping to a straight path for long. Sounds of pursuit reached him, the cries of the demons as they followed his trail, and he redoubled his efforts until all he could hear was his chest heaving and his heart pounding.

He spied a wall ahead, more or less intact, and made his way toward it. He stopped when he came to it, and glanced behind for the first time. The streets were empty all around. There were some shouts, but more distant than the last he had heard. Perhaps the Shadow Men had turned their pursuit against some of the others. It was just as well, because now that he had stopped he couldn't get himself moving again, the lack of food, water and sleep conspiring to leave him dazed. The muscles in his legs quivered uncontrollably and he fell to one knee.

Once there, his stomach rebelled against him, and he found himself retching. The violence of it was miserable, all the more so because there was nothing in his stomach to bring up but a little bile. Everything ached when he was finally done, and he sobbed to himself as he forced himself back to his feet. He looked around at the surrounding alleys again, and, satisfied that he had lost his pursuers, pulled himself over the wall and fell into what had once been the gardens of some estate.

The mansion was in ruins, the entire roof and most of the top story gone, but he didn't care, and made his way to it. There were a few apple trees still growing on the grounds, and he stopped for a moment to pick some of the small, hard fruit, putting a half-dozen in his shield. He walked into what remained of the building through what he supposed must once have been a grand entryway. He picked his way through the ruins, past the outlines of several rooms, until he found a spot in the jostle of broken stones that he thought looked safe.

It was hidden from the view of anyone who might happen through the grounds and the building—only a thorough search would lead to his discovery, and it was more or less safe from the sun. He set his back against the wall and slid down with a sigh, putting his shield to one side and laying his spear across his knees. The apples had started to turn and were bitter and sour, but he ate them all with a growing joy.

25

The days for Masiph passed without incident, five since the ambush and the slaughter of his quadra. Days he would stay in this room tending to Nustef, sleeping when he could manage and listening to the Shadow Men when they came to collect water, as though he might divine from their garbled tongue some idea as to their intentions. Nights he got water from the well, fruit from the trees, and explored the ruins. There was another garden with some fruit trees off one the fallen wings, which meant that he would not lack for food for some time.

He had gone no farther than the walls of the complex, though he had spent a great deal of time peering out onto the surrounding streets. They were always empty, and he had nearly convinced himself that the Shadows did not patrol in the vicinity, otherwise he would have to have seen some of them passing this way on their rounds. It was only a matter of time before he strayed outside the confines to the streets and beyond to see what lay there. If he knew where the Shadows were, where they patrolled and where their lines were, he could try to navigate through them to where the army was camped, if they had not already abandoned the city.

Time was an enemy now. Nustef grew worse each day. For a time it had looked as though the wound was healing, but an infection had set in and now the gash refused to close over. It exuded little blood, but the skin around it was inflamed and swelled at times with a foul-colored pus. Masiph cut it free and cleaned the wound as often as he could, replacing it with dressing he had washed in the well water. He did not know enough about healing to say if he was doing right or wrong by his friend. Without herbs and medicines there was little he could do.

After several days of delirium, during which he raved and moaned, Nustef had the day before fallen into a deep slumber from which he had not awakened. Masiph thought his breathing appeared shallower today, which concerned him, though his heartbeat was steady. In some ways, though, it was a relief—he no longer had to worry about him crying loudly at an inopportune moment. There had been times when the Shadows had been below collecting water that Masiph had thought about gagging him to ensure they were not betrayed.

He wrestled with what he should do to be right by his friends and ancestors. Would he have been better off leaving him to the Shadows, rather than having to suffer these long agonies? Making matters worse was that each day that Nustef survived was a day he could not escape and find his way back to the army. He had considered leaving anyway in the hopes of returning with help, but he knew he would never be allowed if he managed to find his way back to the main force.

Gheyuth was no fool. The dry season was fast approaching, and if he thought that any kind of victory was untenable he would call for a retreat sooner rather than later. He would not let his force suffer Waleen's fate, and if Masiph remained here he might very well be left to that doom. A fitting end for an Ad Ezern, Masiph thought, and he tried to imagine his father's expression when he was told the news.

That night he went to the other garden where he had come across some allieu, an herb that he knew healers used on open wounds, though he was not sure what its effect was. It could do no harm at this juncture, he reasoned. The garden was located, as with the one that held the well, between one of the wings opposite his and the main building. It was in an even greater state of disrepair, with the entire upper floor collapsed upon the main one. But Masiph had found a path through after a night of searching, and he set on it again, stepping carefully, for his knee still hurt to put weight on.

The entrance to the garden was gone, the entire wall of the wing having crumbled, and the only way through was a narrow opening created by the collapse, which forced him to slide through on his belly. He tumbled out the other side, misjudging where the stone ended, landing on his head. He sprang to his feet immediately, blinking at the pain and feeling somewhat sheepish, and found himself eye to eye with a Shadow Man.

The moonlight revealed a startled face. Masiph heard a sharp indrawn breath, which was strangled in its throat as the Shadow leapt back from him, flinging its hands up to ward him off. It was all done too quickly, as the Shadow Man got caught in its feet and toppled to the ground. A terrified yelp followed, and Masiph watched as it scrambled back from him, still not comprehending what was happening as it frantically struggled to regain its equilibrium.

He did not hesitate a moment longer. His sword was in his hands and he fell upon the Shadow, driving a blow at its dark head with the pommel. It landed on the Shadow Man's nose, and he could feel it give way under his fist. He hammered down with the sword again, and there was a terrible sound of bone breaking, the Shadow emitting a pitiful cry. Its hands scrabbled against him, tearing at his robes, trying to halt the sword from coming down. He managed to pin one of its arms to the ground, and the other flailed uselessly as he brought his fist down again. Blood and chunks of something more substantial spattered on his mouth, and it wailed. He spat on it in turn, not relenting in his blows. The demon shuddered beneath him, its arms going limp, but he kept going until the only sound coming from it was a slight gurgling at the back of its throat.

He pulled himself free and stood above the Shadow, entranced by it as it twitched and writhed as though sparked by some untethered force. He ran it through with a blade right to the heart, though that did nothing to stop its movement. His face was damp with blood, and he wiped it off with his sleeve. He stepped back from the body, lurching wildly as he did so, just catching himself before he fell.

It took him a moment to regain his equilibrium and become aware of his surroundings. The quiet of the garden seemed ominous to him, and he fled, squeezing back through the stones of the broken wall, returning to the wing where he had secreted himself. He paced the room for a time, walking around Nustef, listening to the unsteady rhythm of his breathing. He was waiting for something to happen, an alarm to be raised, a party to be sent to investigate the Shadow's pitiful cries.

After half an hour had passed, he allowed himself to believe that no one was coming and that he was safe for the time being. The body was still there, though, and by morning someone among the Shadows would realize one of theirs was missing and a search would begin. If the Shadow Man he had killed knew the path to the garden, he had to assume others did as well, which meant it was only a matter of time before the body was discovered. Worse, any search of these ruins would inevitably lead to the discovery of both he and Nustef. He sighed and glanced down at his friend. Really, there was nothing else for it—the body could not be found on the grounds.

He returned to the garden, looking the body over, and glanced at Senteur's heavens, hoping he still had enough hours of darkness left to him. It was exhausting work dragging the limp and broken body through the narrow opening and then out of the ruined wing and the main building to the gate. He was drenched in sweat and bruised by the time he managed it, the first hints of light beginning to show in the sky.

He darted out into the street, looking to see that it was as empty as it appeared. When he was satisfied that it was safe, he went back to the body and dragged it across to the largest and most intact of the three buildings. He brought it as far inside as he could manage before collapsing in exhaustion. As he stood to leave, not willing to tarry any longer with daylight slowly making its presence felt, he looked down at the Shadow Man, taking its features in for the first time. It was younger than he expected, probably younger than himself, with a slighter build. A large piece of the side of its head had broken away under the force of Masiph's blows, and he was able to see the innards of its brain, which he studied with some fascination.

He had taken a few steps away from it when he stopped and came back and saw what had only dimly registered in him initially. The Shadow had no weapon on its person. He hurried back once again to the garden to find it, but when he got there all he found were pieces of skull and hair and earth streaked with blood. He obscured the blood as much as he could, and threw as many of the pieces of skull and hair as he could over the wall before conducting a frenzied search around the garden for a sword or a spear, a weapon of some sort. There was none to be found, and at last the growing light chased him back to the room.

•••

The sun had disappeared beneath the hills to the west of the city by the time Keleprai made his way from the front lines within the walls to where the Qraul's tent had been set up in the midst of the army's encampment. Within the camp the men milled about with a nervous expectancy, eyes on the shrinking horizon around them. This was the way it had been every night in the desert, the soldiers awaiting an attack through the gloaming, only now that anticipation had been driven to an almost fever pitch by the ambush four days before.

Keleprai felt none of it, only a cold and growing fury. He knew the Shadows would not be attacking this evening. Why bother when they could simply hold their positions in the city, continuing to draw them into battles where they held the advantage? It would only be a matter of time before the men would lose their resolve to continue. Already there were grumblings from Renian hierarchy, and his own kehels would start soon enough. Even the mercenary companies would lose their will once they thought the risk to their lives outweighed that of the coin they would forfeit in leaving the fight. It might get very lonely for them here in the desert soon.

The attendants idling in the outer compartment of the Qraul's tent erupted with a frenzy of concern as he stepped in from the dusk. He waved them aside curtly and stepped into the council room where Cepedutherupt had set up their command. The High Adept was at a table engrossed in some ancient maps of the city his Disciple had brought from the Empire. This had occupied his days since the two armies had entered the city. Laterala was there as well, lying back on a couch, though he sprang to his feet when he saw Keleprai, concern evident in his eyes.

"Do you mean to spend the rest of your Godsforsaken days looking at those maps?"

The High Adept glanced up at Keleprai with a raised eyebrow, apparently only just becoming aware that he had entered the council room. "You should have your head attended to," he said.

Keleprai laughed. "I'll be fine. I'll last long enough to fall under their swords again."

"Keleprai," Laterala said carefully, "I really think you should have someone look at that wound."

Keleprai stared at the young Qraul, and Laterala took a step back, as if he were uncertain what the Gver might do.

"They're going to leave us to our doom."

"Who is that?" Cepedutherupt said in a mild voice, his eyes back on the map.

"The Renians. The Enir."

"I very much doubt it. The companies have too much money still owed to them to risk leaving now. And the Renians. Well, I'm sure Husem Gheyuth will continue to insist we pull out of the city."

"He's right. We can't possibly hold our positions for more than a few days. If Ludenn's men can't hold out, we'll be flanked. And how could they? No food or water. No hope of rescue. Our only choice is to fall back and draw the fight to open ground."

The High Adept stood up from the table to face Keleprai. "As I've said, we must hold this ground. I need time. The goal here is not to defeat the Shadows—they rather outnumber us, as I'm sure you're well aware. We are here to destroy their alkemya."

"We all serve you, turn and turn again," Keleprai said, a surge of bile nearly choking him. "We are all at your service; even our very breath will fill your lungs if need be. And you offer not a bauble in return, but doom. Have you dreamed a way out of it yet? Have you scried our fortunes, or is Senteur's night dark?"

Cepedutherupt did not reply. He stared at Keleprai emanating a kind of serene calm that the Gver found disturbing. He turned to the Qraul, seized by an overwhelming urge.

"This war is folly. I should never have agreed." He stopped and blinked in confusion, a wave of dizziness assaulting him, along with a familiar nausea. It passed, and he continued headlong. "We have to pull out of the city. Pull out completely while there is still a chance. This is madness. We have to get out of the desert."

He expected to see relief cross Laterala's face, in the same way that he felt relief having finally said it, after keeping those words clenched between his grinding teeth these last five days. Instead, the Qraul looked at him with a mixture of terror and worry.

"You're not well, Keleprai," Cepedutherupt said, some urgency in his voice now. "You need to have you head attended to."

"Are you so completely baubleless that you will not act?" he said to Laterala. "You had best hope your wife fills her cellar while you are gone; she'll get no harvest from you."

An attendant Keleprai had not even noticed standing near the Qraul gasped at his words. His sight flickered briefly and then returned, everything a jumble of color and darkness. A swell of nausea clenched him, and he glanced at Cepedutherupt, taking a step toward him.

"What have you done?" he demanded, trying to focus his eyes on the High Adept, a task made difficult as the dizziness returned and began to buzz in his head, the nausea that followed nearly doubling him over. It sounded incredibly loud, like a long clap of thunder, with Cepedutherupt's response a distant murmur of wind coming down from the hills.

He wheeled around to plead to Qraul: "He is using his alkemya on me. Pull the army out now. End it."

But he could tell that he was not understood. The sound in his head continued to reverberate, growing louder. He yelled something at Laterala again, but it was no use. He somehow pulled himself around to face the High Adept, who it seemed was saying something to him, although he was looking over his shoulder. Keleprai shouted at him, a curse, and reached for his sword. But he did not get it in his hand. Around his feet he could see blood, and he fell to ground.

•••

Masiph watched the slow rise and fall of Nustef's chest. The steady repetition of it fascinated him, the ribs jutting outward and then withdrawing back into the chest. Contrasted with the stillness of the rest of his body, it appeared as the silent functioning of some hidden engine. He imagined an imp within furiously working at the cranks to turn them and manufacture the ebb and flow around it.

He tried to match his own breathing to Nustef's, thinking it might still the endless thunder in his mind, but it only made it louder. He closed his eyes tightly and then opened them. Since his encounter with the Shadow he had not left the room. The only thing he had done was to change Nustef's bandages and drink what water and fruit he had. It had been two days and it was nearly gone. Tonight he would have to find a way to the well and fruit trees, though he suspected the Shadows now had guards everywhere.

They were searching for the killer, he was certain. They still came three times a day for water, but there was a difference now, at least to his ears. The joviality he had heard earlier was gone. They knew a murderer was somewhere in their midst in this broken city. His only hope, while he bided his time waiting for a chance to find his way back to the main force, was that they had neither the numbers nor the time to mount a decent search.

Nustef had not woken or stirred in three days. Yesterday Masiph had not been able to get him to swallow any water, and food was impossible. The pus from his wound grew uglier, and the stench was awful. Masiph could not bear to think of what would come next.

Chatter below alerted him to the arrival of the Shadows for their midday water collection. He had difficulty distinguishing them, but it seemed as though there were more than usual. There was fear in their voices, that his ears detected, at least, and he smiled a bit at that. Let them think about the specters that lay hidden and threatening around them. Let them taste their own sweat as they lay down at night.

He listened to the garble below, and though he had no way of knowing what they were saying, he began to think that he did understand the nature of the conversation. They knew he was in the vicinity, and he would be discovered. It was a matter of time. They would find him. There were stories of what happened to Renians captured by the Shadows, the slow tortures they devised. Best not put into thought, let alone dwelled upon.

He did not take his eyes from Nustef, the rise and fall of his chest still mesmerizing, as he asked, "What should we do? What should we do?"

"The devourer of all lies beneath us. It will rise up and feast on our blood and marrow."

Masiph felt the breath go still in his chest. He closed his eyes and willed the realms quiet.

"This realm is spoiled. It tastes foul, and when the devourer is through with the sweet, the rotten will be spat forth."

"Yes," Masiph said, "we are ruined beyond cure."

26

"You and I, we see things differently," Fenar said to Donier as he led him down the empty street. "There is no point in finding our way back. This is the end of times, and we are here to witness the birth here at the end of all realms."

Donier grunted noncommittally as he scanned the abandoned city ahead of them for signs of the Shadows. He had not encountered any since his flight two days before, and he assumed that he was far enough north in the city—the spires of what he took to be the Gver's palace were visible to the south—to be away from the front lines and their camps. They had to be getting supplies from somewhere, though, most likely from the north, and they had to pass through the streets somewhere with them.

Fenar, who claimed to have been wandering this area alone since the first attack, also claimed not to have seen a Shadow Man since, and was in fact quite convinced that they would not come across any on their sojourn. Donier found this conviction hard to square with the man's apocalyptic worldview, but consistency of belief did not appear to be among his concerns. *We are all choirs, not soloists, anyway*, Donier told himself. His father had been fond of that phrasing.

"A fearsome beast shall rise from within this very earth that we are standing upon, swimming through the land like a whale. Ulternon's final creation, to wreak havoc upon his whoresons and their realms. All that will be left is ruins and desert such as this. The totality." Fenar shouted the last words, causing Donier to wince and look about to see if anything had stirred.

They had stumbled across each other the day after his escape from the mausoleum, as he set off to get himself farther from where he assumed the Shadow Men were positioned. He had filled his shield with apples, most of them rotting and picked at by birds, but food nonetheless, and ate them as he went. His stomach was troubled by the fruit, but he kept eating them, even if just to keep some moisture working in his mouth, which was so dry he feared it would begin to bleed.

Fenar had been singing, and Donier crept upon him, suspecting some sort of a trap, but instead he found a man sitting on a stone beneath the shade of an orange tree, peeling one of its fruits. He wondered if he might be hallucinating somehow, for though he now had some food in his belly, he still had not been able to sleep. He could almost believe what Fenar said, for everything looked out of sorts, a blurring edge that might portend doom of some sort.

"The beast, a caterpillar as lustful in appetites as any common trull, shall come forth in the next three days and feast upon the spirit of all those in this city. A quenching supper. Then it shall set forth to lay waste to this realm, and the fairer one above ruled by his master's brother starling." Fenar continued on in this vein for some time, and Donier did his best to ignore him.

As they were walking, Donier spied another fruit tree, with what looked like pears heavy on its limbs, within the walls of a ruined estate. He led the way through the gaping entrance and past the crumbling edifice to the scrub-overgrown garden presided over by the lone tree. The pears were just past their ripeness, but he found a few that were good and sat on a nearby stone to eat them. Fenar picked a few as well, whistling now, and then sat across from him and continued laying forth the decimation that would be brought forth by the beast of Ulternon.

Donier interrupted him before he could go any further. "Why would Ulternon want to destroy all realms?"

Fenar looked startled at the question, as if he had just assumed that Donier was paying him no mind. "Well...it is clear. It's not just Ulternon, but Melinon. You see, the Senteurists...the brother starling is winning the war. He will triumph. But the others will not allow it. Melinon would rather an empty cellar and broken keep than one ruled by him."

Donier wiped his mouth of juice and tried to smother a grin.

"And what are the signs, exactly? A palanquin moving with ushers? A salamander afire?"

"Everywhere, everywhere. You cannot comprehend. The Senteurists have control of court. The boy Qraul, his mother is one of them, and it has infected the whole court. Just think of this war we are in here. What purpose does it have? Think of it. We are not here to conquer, then what?"

Donier shrugged. Who was he to say?

"You see, you see, you do not know and you a second."

"We know no more than any of the common soldiers." Another shrug, and he bit deeply into another pear.

For some reason this made Fenar laugh, and he slapped his knee. "Yes, nobody knows anything for sure, do they. The Gods are mysterious and obscure."

"They must be working pretty plainly for you to know all this."

"Maybe so, maybe so. My eyes are clear to the signs. I have been invited to see. The Senteurists have poisoned the court of the Qraul and they have taken us into this war. And it is this which is the trigger: the earth will tremble beneath our feet and the beast shall follow in the path Ulternon has crafted for it."

Donier decided he'd had enough, and got to his feet, not even looking to see if Fenar followed. Part of him hoped that he wouldn't, but of course there he was, falling in step, continuing to expound on the end of all realms. Donier concluded that he would have to make serious considerations as to how to get rid of this fool. The constant ruckus he was creating would eventually draw the attention of the Shadows before he managed to find water and return to the main army outside Esyln.

The day was drawing to a close, and their wanderings had proven to be in vain, when Donier decided to abandon the search for a well and find somewhere to lie down for the night. They found what he imagined had once been a temple, with a lone entrance, which they managed to block off with some stones. Mercifully, once they had sealed the entrance, Fenar lay down and promptly fell asleep, sparing him any further theological disquisitions.

Donier was too restless to sleep, and instead ate some more of the fruit he had gathered, hoping it would settle his mind. Sleep continued to evade him, though, and his night passed, filled with waking visions. Again and again he saw himself wandering alone in the desert valley, empty of any other creatures. Every so often he would start and open his eyes, convinced that some part of his vision, an outcropping of rocks or a cacti that lay on the edge of the imagining, was in fact a Shadow moving toward him through the darkness. But the darkness stayed constant around him, the silence marred only by the light snoring of Fenar.

They found a well first thing the next morning when Fenar stepped into a nearby courtyard to relieve himself. He yelled over the wall at Donier, who had been contemplating whether he should use this opportunity to make his escape. Instead he ran, almost falling over himself as he did so, to where Fenar squatted, his robes still pulled up about his hips, and saw the well in the corner in seemingly good repair. The pump worked easily and the water came quickly, tumbling to the ground, sweet and glorious. They both laughed in wonder, gorging themselves on it before filling their canteens.

Donier felt transformed. The ache at the back of his head disappeared as they drank. For the first time in days he felt somewhat whole, his soul and his being no longer fractured, the edges to his vision no longer blurred and threatening. The Gods were on his side, he decided, freeing him from his doom at the mausoleum, bringing him to this water here. Now he had only to find his way back to the army and all would be well.

When they had well and truly sated themselves, they returned to the street. Just as they did, a band of Shadow Men turned onto it, emerging right in front of them. Donier whirled around to run, only to be faced by a half-dozen more spears leveled at his neck. His mouth, so gloriously wet just moments before, had gone dry. Fenar began to speak about Ulternon and the unleashing of the beast.

"You see, here we have sign," he said. "Here is a sign indeed."

The Shadow nearest knocked him to the ground with a blow from his sword. Fenar moaned, blood on his lips. Donier watched in amazement as they kicked him hard in the ribs. One of them bent over Fenar and tore his shield and spear from his hands and the sword from his belt, while the others stood poised, ready to strike should Fenar resist.

As Donier watched disbelieving, wondering why they were not killing Fenar, one of the Shadows jabbed him with a spear. Donier turned to look, and the Shadow Man said something, gesturing with his weapon. Donier dropped his spear and shield to the ground, and then undid his belt and tossed his sword aside. Someone from behind kicked his knees out. Once he was on the ground, the Shadow facing him stepped forward and struck him in head and he felt darkness descend around him.

FOUR:

DANCE OF THE SHADOWS

27

Two mercenaries walked ahead, their lanterns held aloft in one hand, swords in the other. Two walked behind Vyissan by a few steps with lantern and sword, while two others marched at pace with him with crossbows armed and ready to fire. His sword was at his side, and he had a copy of the map given him by the emperor open in his hands that he squinted down at through the lamplight. There was a quid in his mouth and two more in his pouch, which he hoped would be enough to last him on this journey through the depths of the desert.

In the end, neither he nor Cepedutherupt had managed to ferret out the entrance to the labyrinth. One of the cohorts had discovered it in the camp without even realizing what it was. A soldier harvesting cactus for their water and inner flesh had found one growing at an odd angle, from beneath a rock, and a closer investigation had revealed a hollow beneath.

Its origins were difficult to discern, for the tunnel had collapsed, earth filling in much of the entryway. The cohorts had used it to bury their dead. There was no wood to be spared for pyres, and the rock the camp was situated on made digging graves nearly impossible. Using the hole seemed a happy solution—certainly better than leaving the bodies to the demons and the tolotes.

Vyissan, on his way out to continue his futile search at first light, had watched in amazement as two soldiers emerged from the earth and then crouched in prayer, throwing some offerings in the hole before leaving. The Gods were laughing at them, clearly, he thought, as he sent word to the High Adept. He spent a rather noxious hour trying to find the entryway, holding a lantern high as two mercenaries dug at the walls while trying not to retch. He could only imagine what the Enir must be thinking at the sacrilege being done to the Craitolian ancestors here, improperly buried and now being disturbed so soon in their rest.

Only a few splintered pieces of wood remained along with some broken stone, of whatever door had once existed there. How much of the tunnel was collapsed, Vyissan wondered, knowing they might have to dig for days to reach a usable section, time they did not have. He was just about to retreat above, to fresher air, and to find some more mercenaries to help with the excavation when one of the Enir let out a muted shout of triumph, his shovel sliding through to empty air beyond. As they kept digging, a breeze began to stir from below, the air sweet and pure.

By midday, he and the five mercenaries started on their way. The only noise was the broken rhythm of their footsteps; the rest was a musty silence made ominous by the encroaching gloom. They did not speak, though Vyissan could sense everyone's nervousness, which matched his own. The darkness, combined with the narrow corridors and the unknown that awaited them beyond their lanterns' glow, conspired to create a feeling of a fist clamping down around him—a ridiculous sensation, but one that was palpably real. At one point a lantern flickered out, casting the shadows even deeper, leading to one of the men gasping in shock. Vyissan was not entirely certain it had not been him.

He had the map to guide them, but it was unnecessary—the dim flicker of the quicksilver's astral, as it was shaped into alkemy by the Shadows who manned the engines, became an omnipresent throb that worked at his temples, filling him with dread at the confrontation that awaited him. The Enir mercenaries could feel it as well, and Vyissan could sense their growing disquiet at the foreign sensations they were feeling. It would only grow worse the closer they got to the engines.

When they had first entered the labyrinth, he had not felt the engines and had briefly allowed himself to hope that the High Adept had been wrong, his agents among the Shadow Men misinforming him, and that the engines and the Shadows' false Adepts were elsewhere in the city. As soon as he felt the first twinge of astral, and scented the faint singed smell that touched the air, he knew that there would be no avoiding this battle, though he found himself imagining leading the mercenaries astray and losing their way in the labyrinth's tunnels.

And then what? Wait for the Shadows to stumble upon them? There was no escaping his fate now.

One of the men leading the way coughed loudly, and it echoed down the corridor, causing them all to freeze, as though they expected the Shadow Men to emerge from the stillness that followed. None did, which Vyissan supposed was not a surprise, given most of the Shadows would be above ground or guarding the engines. The tunnels smelled of absence and decay, empty of everything but for the darkness, ever expanding beyond their sight, like Senteur's heavens without the stars to fill them. All the realms unborn here.

It did not seem they had been walking long, though it must have been for hours, when they came upon a wall that blocked their path. Vyissan swore and consulted the map and then looked it over again, but he could find no error in his navigation. He put aside the map and took a lantern from one of the soldiers, casting its glow across the wall. There was no doorway secreted within its frame that he could see, nor any places where time had done its work to fray its strength.

The mercenaries joined him beside it. One of them ran his hand along it, almost caressing the stone.

"Looks newer than the rest of this," he said.

Vyissan nodded, lifting the lantern high to look at where the ceiling and the wall met. "Yes."

"Think maybe the Shadows put it here?"

"It would make sense." Vyissan nodded.

"Is that the plan, then?" another mercenary said. "We use these against them, send the army through and attack them from below?"

Vyissan stepped away from the wall and sent an image to the High Adept. "Something like that."

"If they used them before, then likely they're still down in here somewhere," the first Enir said.

"Oh, I'm certain they are," Vyissan said. "We are planning on it. It will be their downfall."

The mercenaries looked doubtful of this, but Vyissan ignored them. An image came to him, the sun setting above, them below in the tunnels, at the wall, lying down to sleep. He replied with the same image, only this time the sun was coming up. Cepedutherupt's reply was immediate—the wall lay broken, and they passed beyond. The quicksilver flowing blue-silver through the carefully shaped glass tubes awaited him there. It was not in the image, but his mind supplied it all the same.

The men were staring at him, he realized. He cleared his throat. "We stay here for the night."

Their relief was evident. "Do we look for another route through tomorrow?" one of them asked.

"There is no other route," he said.

"What, then?"

"Tomorrow we go through."

One of the men, he saw, made a warding sign against him.

•••

Darkness still held sway as Phariayh returned to the camps where the armies remained on the edge of the ruined city. This was her second foray into the camp, after a few miserable days in solitude trying to subsist on roots and cactus flowers had resulted in her spending most of her time squatting to relieve herself while cursing her own stupidity. The first time she had made off with enough food—bread, cheese, ardeh milk and even some cured meat—to last her for two days, which she had spent in the flat wasteland south of the city where the only beings she had encountered were a few tolotes and the usual desert birds.

No one was awake in the Renian encampment, except a few of the wounded, who moaned and offered muttered invocations to their ancestors, but Phariayh kept her distance from them, heading to where the sutlers had their supply wagons. There were guards, of course, as well as the sentries, but she had no issue avoiding them. The sentries had their eyes upon the city, for they knew that was where the Shadows were, and the guards were men hired by the sutlers who spent the greater part of their evenings drinking mehcuil. By this time of the night, with morning only an hour away, most were asleep.

As before, she moved at an angle between the Craitolian and Renian camps. Both armies had established themselves at a careful distance from the other, not quite trusting their allies, but neither force had been willing to make more visible their distrust by setting guards against each other. Which meant that once Phariayh had slipped by the Craitolian sentries, she had a clear path to the center of the Renian camp where the sutlers were.

The darkness was thinning as she went, the first hints of the sunrise to come, and she could just make out the vast tent of Craitol's Ad Eselte. She wondered briefly about the emissary and what he was doing at that moment. Had he found the cauldron he feared was his fate, or was he within the tent, wondering what had become of her? It did not matter, she knew—her own fate lay elsewhere. Each day she survived now seemed a miracle, and she gave praise to her ancestors, not daring to think about what would happen to her once the army began its march back to Darrhyn. Could she stalk the army across the desert, scavenging from it what she needed? Unlikely, but she would meet that day when it came.

The ardehs stirred as she slipped by them, but Phariayh did not pause, moving confidently, as though she were meant to be there. She felt her pulse begin to quicken as she came to the wagons, excited at the thought of once again stealing food from under the noses of those who had tried to murder her. In these moments she could almost believe that she might be able to survive as the army journeyed back across the desert. She had no need of the emissary's protection, or the pity of anyone. She could survive on her own.

Between her thoughts and her excitement, Phariayh did not hear the muffled grunting until it was too late, and she found herself face to face with one of the girls who had been indentured to Fush. The girl was bent over the supply wagon, her robes pulled up around her hips, her eyes closed and her mouth bent into a wordless grimace. One of the guards was behind her, accentuating each of his thrusts into her with a soft grunt.

Phariayh stared at them, unable to move, and watched in horror as the girl opened her eyes and saw her through the shadows. She screamed in terror, seeming not to recognize Phariayh, and jumped away from the wagon, setting the guard off balance and sprawling to the ground. The girl did not even look at him, turning and fleeing as fast as she could, screaming at the top of her lungs that there were Shadows in the camp.

The camp was transformed from quiet stillness to tumult and cacophony in a matter of moments following the girl's screams. Sentries around both the Renian and Craitolian camps sounded the alarm, and all the quadras within rose as one, seemingly, weapons in hand, looking about for the Shadow Men threat. The guard by Phariayh scrambled to his feet as well, looking around wildly, before spotting her. He did recognize her, and he snarled and called out, "The beast is here to steal our food."

Phariayh turned and ran blindly through the sutlers' tents, knocking aside a few of the girls who had risen from the ground they slept on to see what the cause of the commotion was. The sulihers, hearing the screams of the women, turned within and began to move to the camp's center, straining through the darkness to see the Shadows who had somehow slipped within. Fortunately, they did not see her, and she was able to make her way back the way the way she had come, in the emptiness between the two camps.

She was almost beyond both camps when two Craitolian sentries spotted her and moved to intercept. Phariayh turned heel and ran back through the gap in the camps, sulihers from both armies still confused and slow to respond. Pursuit came eventually, and she could hear the heavy steps and the clank of armor as the sulihers strained to catch her. They did not, though, and they would not, she realized. She was quick and light where they were slow, and she had enough of a head start that she passed between both camps with ease.

She did not stop, though the air now burned in her lungs and her legs had begun to ache, running without heed toward the city. The sounds of pursuit slowly died as she ducked through a hole in the city wall and dodged among the ruined buildings, the sulihers not wanting to risk being drawn into some manner of trap. When the only footsteps she could hear were her own, Phariayh wriggled through a crevice created by the collapse of a building and crawled through the scattered stones until the space around her opened up and she found herself in the remnants of a room.

There were holes in the roof, and, as she lay there trying to gather her breath and collect her thoughts, she watched as the stars disappeared from the sky.

•••

It was late in the day when Masiph finally stirred from where he lay and went to crouch over Nustef's still form. The stench from the wound had grown ever more putrid; now it seemed as though it was a third presence inhabiting the air between their more solid forms. Masiph had left the room several times, going to see if the stench was evident beyond its walls, and he thought he could detect a faint note of decay.

"Not long," he whispered, and brought his face level with Nustef's prone form. "Not long at all."

He coughed and spat on the floor, breathing heavily through his mouth, and thought for some reason of fat gone rancid. The Shadows would be arriving soon to get water for the evening. The heat of the day could only have made the stench worse, and who knew how far it might have spread? It was insidious. He could feel it in the pores of the skin on his face. If they came to this wing to investigate, as surely they must soon, with the dead Shadow's killer still about, then they would not fail to notice the smell and he would be discovered.

In a way he looked forward to that moment, longed for its arrival. He hadn't determined yet what he would do when they came. A final stand would be the noble thing, an act to praise his ancestors before he entered their embrace, but he was not sure that he had the stomach for it just now.

Nustef had told him of the devourer of all working beneath the city, and there were times when he thought he could feel its movements as it gathered its strength and prepared to emerge. The desert sages had spoken of red rains to come with the end of times, and he wondered if this heat might be a prelude to that. The rains were almost over, though, the dry season to come. But such things did not matter at the end of times. The seasons would be out of joint, just as time, and all the elements would be.

"Maybe this is not the end," he said tentatively to Nustef. "Maybe this is just…this is the beginning. When things end, something else begins, no? So maybe this is the beginning. Everything will go ahead from now."

Nustef did not reply, and Masiph thought that, no, he was fooling himself, just grasping at whatever comfort his mind would give him in this terrible moment.

"We can't stay," he said at last, his voice sounding raw and frightened. He listened for a moment to the stillness of the afternoon beyond the room, hardly a breeze stirring and only a few birds chattering in the gardens below. He choked back a sob and put his head in his hands. Regaining his composure, he stood and walked away from Nustef, staring out the doorway down the empty, disintegrating corridor.

"No," he said at last. "You are right. We can't stay. Tonight, after they've come for the water, we'll go."

He turned back to where Nustef lay, nodding at him, and went to lie down, trying to sleep. When he closed his eyes, he could hear someone singing. It sounded as if it was coming from the street, but it was a Renian voice. The song was familiar, like the hint of some spice in a quid that he couldn't place. He opened his eyes and the singing went away, and when he asked Nustef if had heard anything, he got no reply.

"Tonight," he said. "Tonight we'll go."

The sound of his voice made him start, and he blinked, looking around and trying to recall what he had said. He saw Nustef, a pitiful sight now. He couldn't stand to look for long, and he lay back down and closed his eyes to wait for evening and the Shadows to come.

That night they did not.

•••

Vyissan called a halt at midday, and they set the lanterns down and ate some food. The corridors had both widened and grown more numerous, with passages branching off in a multitude of directions, above and below and around. It required a more careful eye than it had yesterday to navigate their way through the maze, and he had spent the morning with his whole being focused on the map in his hands, paying little mind to the passing labyrinth. The mercenaries with him remained intent on the surrounding darkness that, since they had gone through the wall that morning, seemed more insidious, creeping within the circle of light cast out by their lanterns.

One of the lanterns flickered out, leading to a flutter of nervousness amongst the mercenaries. There was some fumbling and panic with the lantern as the Enir struggled to get it lit, all to no end, for the Shadows failed to materialize out of the darkness. As yet they had found no traces of the Shadow Men in the corridors of the labyrinth, no sign of them ever having been there, even as the pulse of the engines thrummed upon Vyissan's temple. It was enough to make him wonder if these men were ghosts, spirits from another realm, though the soldiers above had proof enough that the Shadows were flesh. They had tasted the bite of their swords.

It was his success or failure, Vyissan knew, that would determine whether those losses had meaning or not. Though if the soldiers above, the mercenaries especially, had an inkling of what the war was really about, they might consider the whole thing pointless, regardless of the outcome. Vyissan could not disagree. It was not theirs to decide, though, nor was it his.

When they had sated their appetites and rested as best they could manage, Vyissan ordered them forward again. They were nearing wherever the engines had been hidden, and he suspected they would be there in a little more than an hour. Their effect was growing more profound. It felt like a dozen Adepts and their Disciples working in concert at once. His head ached at the alkemy at play as the unseen battle was waged between the Council's Adepts and the Shadows' engines.

The men with him were beginning to feel its effects as well. He could tell from the stray hands that wandered to their temples and the questioning looks they cast about. None dared speak—he imagined they wanted to, but they feared alerting the Shadows. When they caught his eye he tried to look reassuring, a difficult thing to manage under the circumstances. He saw more than one warding sign cast furtively by free hands.

They walked an hour, probably more, encountering nothing. The mercenaries' faces shone with sweat from the strain. Vyissan had stopped worrying. If it came it came, but he did not think anything would happen. A serene knowing had seized him, and he felt confident that they would make it to the engines without issue. The Gods had chosen. What befell them there he could not say, but he would set his eyes upon them. He would be given the opportunity to strike the decisive blow.

It was only a few minutes later that one of the men in the lead coughed, asking a wordless question. Vyissan drew his eyes up from the map and looked at what lay ahead at the light's edge. They were still some distance from where the labyrinth connected with the palace, which was where he assumed the Shadows had positioned the engines. What he saw told a different tale.

There was a hole in the middle of the corridor, with stairwells descending on either side of the gap. It was not on the map. He grabbed one of the lanterns and took a cautious step forward to the stair's edge, lifting it high to illuminate what was below. He couldn't see to the bottom, but it was clear that the stairs were a new addition to the labyrinth. They were made from the same hard earthen mixture that the Renians had used in places, but the coloring was different.

A fresh wave of nausea assailed him. The air felt like it was moving up the stairs and passing right through him, as though he was immaterial and it the substance. Perhaps in this state he was. In its wake, his knees and hands started to ache and throb with heat, as if the process of his own combustion had begun. The stench of burning resin that was used to animate the engines did little to dissuade this feeling.

He glanced back at the mercenaries, and saw by their expressions that they wanted to go anywhere but down the stairs into that pit of alkemya. He set his face hard and folded the map, putting it away, hoping this wouldn't be the moment when his nausea would overwhelm him. He sent an image of stairwell to the High Adept, and then, with a final glance behind, set off down the stairs.

28

It was as much by feel as by sight that Vyissan realized he had reached the end of the stairway. He set aside the lamp, having extinguished it halfway down the stairs after realizing how brazenly stupid it was to be broadcasting his presence to whoever awaited him below, and turned around to see if the mercenaries had followed. It was with immense relief that he saw them huddling behind him, though he suspected they would make little difference in this endgame. Their faces were etched with fear in the dim light of the unseen engines' slight glow, as, he imagined, was his. He turned while his will still held and led them forward.

There was a long corridor leading off the stairway which he picked his way along, the pathway somewhat illuminated by the silvery-blue glow of the quicksilver from the engines. The mercenaries were whispering invocations to their ancestors, and he glared at them to be silent, though he could not resist uttering his own plea to the Gods for mercy. There was a rumble from the engines, not a sound exactly, but a pulsing vibration, loud and yet deeply silent simultaneously. It left him with an itch he could not scratch inside his ears, worming its way in deeper and deeper to the core of his being.

The corridor opened into a cavernous room the Shadows had carved out of the existing maze work. Its ceiling, Vyissan guessed, was probably level with the top of the stairwell they had just descended, and the space within could have held a hundred men comfortably. Opposite to the entrance, engines were stacked along the wall on scaffolding, rising halfway to the roof. The glow from the quicksilver veins was made more unearthly by the heavy smoke emanating from the brazier at the base of the scaffolding. It all served to give the dozen or so Shadow Men on the scaffolding, who were busy shaping the astral produced by the engines into seeds of alkemy, the appearance of sickly monsters.

As he studied them, Vyissan realized that he was seeing not many engines but one apparatus. The engines had all been interconnected in some manner which he could not glean from this distance, their pans removed, replaced by the brazier at the base of the contraption. Two of the Shadows traded off working the bellows that fed air into the brazier, which erupted with swirling clouds of its noxious exhaust, not unlike the whirlwinds he had encountered aboveground in the desert. Had Kercubegahedd's minions ever attempted such a monstrous feat, he wondered as he stared at this thing, which, for the moment, seemed more alive to him than the spectral entities that worked its appendages.

A few other Shadow Men wrestled with a lone engine that sat on the floor apart from the apparatus. Aside from that, the room was bare, and Vyissan wondered why they had constructed so large a chamber when they could barely manage to fill a wall. But then, as the High Adept had continually insisted, it was not the engines they possessed, no matter how grand, that were the danger. Those the Council Adepts could handle, as the last days' struggles had proven. It was the engines they were even now building, that the size of this room anticipated, which made it essential that they stop the Shadows before they grew too powerful.

The mercenaries were absolutely still at his side, their expressions marked with wonder and fear at the contraptions they were seeing for the first time. Vyissan had to admit it was awe-inspiring to see the engines at work, the quicksilver dancing through the carefully shaped tubes so that it would shift in element, from solid to liquid to gas. The shifting of so much quicksilver was destabilizing to any nearby substances: the air, the earth, even the Shadow Men and themselves. That was the reason for the vibration they all felt, the edge of their being giving way to transmutation, the astral of all things yearning to be loosed from its elemental being. It was both awful and thrilling to experience. Awful for the way it made him feel—a deep pit of nausea was even now working its way through him—and thrilling for the astral here to be shaped, more than he could ever hope to draw upon through his own skill.

The Shadows were so engrossed in their tasks that they failed to notice the newcomers in their midst. Vyissan waited for the High Adept to signal to him his readiness, and when it came he turned to the mercenaries.

"Kill the Shadows moving that engine," he whispered to them, surprised at the violence in his voice. "The rest," he added, answering the question he saw in their eyes, "leave to me, unless they attack. It is essential that you protect me and allow me time to do my work."

None of them replied, but they turned and set across the room, two taking up position to guard him against attack, with the other four going to deal with the Shadows around the lone engine. Their movement attracted the eyes of the Shadow Men, and shouts went up among them as they realized there were intruders present. The Shadows on the ground drew their swords and charged at the mercenaries, while the rest turned back to work the engines.

"It must be now," he said aloud, though of course Cepedutherupt could not hear him, and the mercenaries did not understand his tongue. It did not matter, for in that moment, the final battle had begun.

Vyissan worked to form the germ of alkemy, the scaffolding and the Shadow Men disappearing as he did, his mind turned inward. The very air swam with the decayed astral the quicksilver in its simultaneity had drawn forth, so much that even with the dozen Shadows each shaping a germ to direct at the Council Adepts there was still so much spillage that it required no effort to gather it. Vyissan began to shape these remains, even as he was prying other astral from its binds, using his own to draw the rest, to form the embryo of the seed of alkemy.

As he formed the seed, Cepedutherupt seized it. It was a wrenching sensation, like hands prying apart his skull and reaching far within to touch what lay there. Horrifying in a way too, to be faced with the stark fact that, body and soul, he was but a vessel. Whatever power he held was in stead, to be guided by a sterner hand. For a moment he could see nothing—the alkemy surging through and around him was so great that it overwhelmed all his senses. He could taste and smell the transmutation; it was like the ash of a thunder cloud. His eyes swam with color.

Through it all he did not halt his efforts, decaying the astral and forming the germ. It was a thoughtless exercise; he had trained for so long for a moment such as this, now that it was upon him he could act as if controlled by the memory of what he and the High Adept had practiced. The rest of his being had seemingly left his body, standing above even the scaffolding to observe the struggle, which had begun in earnest.

The Shadows now had two forces pressing against them: the Council Adepts and their Disciples, formidable in their alkemya, but who they had been able to match in strength up to now, and the High Adept in the person of his Disciple. The hope being that, with Vyissan's proximity, Cepedutherupt would be able to strike a blow directly at the engines which the Shadows could not parry without opening themselves to destruction from the rest of the Council.

It would need to be a death blow, for their forces on the ground could not hope to overwhelm the Shadow Men. They would be left broken and scattered to crawl back across the desert, hoping only to be granted their lives by the Gods. Vyissan had no such hope if they failed; they would succeed or he would perish here. Even then, his life might be in doubt.

He had no sense of how the battle was going—the stew of alkemy in the air did not seem to change. His own immobility did not help matters. He was a part and yet separate from the proceedings. He could almost imagine them continuing on without him as he slipped back up the stairs, but he knew that was impossible with the High Adept commanding him. His back had begun to throb and his legs were stiff. The room was exceptionally hot, whether from the exertion of the engines or the transmutation of so much astral he could not say, but he was drenched in sweat from it.

How, he wondered, could the balance of the aspects be maintained here, when so much of the astral was being taken leaving only a hollow elemental, a shadow of the thing itself? The Council forbade such actions, but it was always a question of degrees with these things, especially now that events had carried them to this point. One could justify anything in a moment, especially when that moment was laced with doom as this one was. Still, the very fabric of the realms seemed ready to tremble, the air wrenching violently as the struggle persisted. Would there be nothing left? Would they just eat at themselves until there was no astral remaining to the realm while the earth fell in upon them?

There was a tolote nipping at his heels. He tried to turn to confront the creature, but it seemed he was actually lying on the ground. Turning back, he found himself facing the crystal blue of the empty desert sky. He tried to kick at the tolote, but it was no use, and the creature moved to his face and began to gnaw at his eyes.

There was frantic movement among the Shadows on the scaffolding. The smell of the engines and the resin was much worse. He felt nauseous and longed to vomit. He was forced to stand instead, with the feeling sitting in his stomach, a heavy pit, deeper the farther in one went. He crawled in choosing the corridors and byways at random, blinking away at the bile as it ebbed and flowed blue and silver, until he lost his way and settled down to bide his time.

The ceremony was the first time Vyissan had laid eyes upon the High Adept. The Council had only announced their joining the day before, but they were moving quickly to unite them Adept to Disciple. Cepedutherupt's old Disciple had taken to bed and seemed unlikely to recover, and the High Adept of the Realm could not be long without his adherent. These were still trying times, after all, the peace of the Realm as delicate as ever.

It had surprised him that he had been chosen for such an honor, given his heritage. There were those among the Council, and especially among his cohort, who viewed him with suspicion or worse because of the shade of his skin. The war against the northern insurrectionists was still ongoing, though in the shadows. Perhaps that had been enough to disqualify him from being named an Adept, but none could deny his talent. To be chosen by the High Adept was the culmination of all he had dreamed of in those days before he had come south to see what destiny the Gods had shaped for him.

He did not remember the ceremony, the prayers to the Gods, the incense burned, the blood given. All of deep significance, all empty gestures compared to what followed. The linking of two souls, those long hours sitting without stirring in that silent room, the summer heat heavy and still, even his sweat immobile, trapped between his robes and his body. They were near enough to touch sitting across from each other, though they both had their eyes closed in meditation, only the High Adept's breathing indicating his presence to Vyissan. He matched his own to Cepedutherupt's steady rhythm, and his body lost all sensation. He felt as if he were floating off the floor, only that constant rhythm left to guide him.

One was not supposed to think during meditation, but thoughts came unbidden, flitting across the darkness he had cast himself in. He thought of the journey that had brought him to this moment, all that he had strived and longed for. And, in spite of himself, he thought of the two Disciples who had come before him, one now suddenly taken to bed, older than his years, the other perished under mysterious circumstances in the northern war.

Finally the rhythm became omnipresent, and the cacophony of his mind fell silent next to his exhalations. Awareness dawned next, awareness such that he had not known he was capable. He saw himself, both astral and elemental, and he saw the High Adept in those same elements. It was one of the strange ironies of alkemya that the greatest crime against the Council and the practice of alkemya, the taking of another's astral, was also central to the highest ceremony, the joining of Adept to Disciple. That was what he did now, taking some of the astral essence of the High Adept, even as he felt his own essence being taken. They formed a seed of alkemy together, a delicate and fragile thing, which, even as it flickered into being, began its decomposition, leaving their essences intermingled, a link forged.

In that moment, he knew the High Adept as few would ever know another. And yet it was an empty knowing, not the knowing of a lover or a friend. There was no feeling associated with it, at least none he felt. In that moment they were equals, though, neither more nor less. But moments never last, time goes ever forward as the Gods will it, and one must always submit and one will always command.

Vyissan came to with a gasp. The pain had been so great that he had left himself briefly, though somehow he remained standing. His nausea was gone, the aches and burning of his muscle and bone as well. What was left was a nothing, a shuddering emptiness. He seemed to be floating, there and not there, watching, but helpless to move. And the emptiness, the nothing, was absolute, it was everywhere within him, expanding and contracting until there was nothing else but its pulsation.

A distant bell of agony, sounding out a slow rhythm. He blinked, looking for it, but saw only the strewn bodies of the Shadows. How had they come to be that way? There were a few left on the scaffolding. He noticed one was a Kragian half-breed, the white and the dark coalescing across its face. *Demons. Creatures.* The tolote was at his heels again. The half-breed was staring at him in a knowing way, as if he could see through the coloring that Vyissan still wore. *Atasem den Adessel.*

There was a blinding flash as the air turned to fire all around him. There were screams. He wondered if one of them was his own, but he thought not. There was nothing left of him that was able to scream. It was very difficult to breathe; his lungs seemed to be engulfed, and the heat and pain were so great he passed out again, only to jar awake as a new wave of fire surged around him.

The engines started to burst, sending out streams of quicksilver and glass and whoever among the Shadows had managed to survive the flames perished then. Vyissan had a strange urge to flee, thwarted by his leaden body, the astral still being drawn to him, the alkemy forced through, his aspect torn from him. He was terrified of what would be left when it finally stopped, for the emptiness was still there somewhere within, moving. He would have to face that abyss yet.

29

The irons sitting exposed to the afternoon sun had grown hot to the touch, and a bit of shifting restlessness while he dozed caused Donier to flinch awake. He opened one eye to look out on the scene, and saw that it was much as it had been when he had slumped to the ground to sleep earlier that morning. There were more than a dozen of them chained together, including Fenar and himself. Renians and Craitolians in equal parts and two Shadows as well. They had been left to rest on the desert rock while their guards had retreated to watch over them from the relative shade of a nearby dala tree. There were a few other trees beyond that one, and the rest of the force had set their tents in amongst them.

The engines lay nearby, within his purview from where he lay. He had known what they were as soon as he had laid eyes on them the day before. There was nothing else those glass monstrosities could be—he had never seen their like before, had only heard stories, but the eerie silver-blue of the quicksilver was immediately identifiable. They looked lightweight, fragile almost, sitting there now, but he knew that appearance was false.

The engines, tied down onto wooden frames, had first appeared in their midst sometime during that long day and night after their capture. After they had regained consciousness, they were led to a courtyard in what he guessed had been the Gver's palace, now the site of furious activity. Shadow Men came and went, many carrying packs, which seemed to Donier to indicate they were either leaving on or arriving from a long journey. He drifted in and out of consciousness and agony from the beating as he lay in their midst watching their machinations, unable to comprehend what they were about.

They kicked him and the others awake in the dead of night, giving them some water and a bit of stale flat bread made from a grain he did not recognize. Then they were forced to carry the engines on carriages that they hoisted on their shoulders, four of them chained together for each carriage holding two of the engines. They made slow progress through the rest of the night and into the morning, making their way out of the city to the north and into the hills that surrounded the city. Sometime near midday the demons called a halt and the carriers set aside their load and collapsed to the fitful sleep he had just awoken from.

His stomach rumbled sharply, and he raised himself up halfway to a sitting position, looking every which way. The irons rattled as he moved, drawing a cursory glance from the Shadows under the tree. The sound made him shiver, as it had all through the forced march. There was a sort of doom in that noise. A fate worse than death, was the thought that occurred, and this might prove to be it.

None of the others with him were awake, and there was no stirring around the tents that he could see. One of the Shadows beneath the tree leaned forward and spat out whatever it was it had been chewing, its eyes locking on Donier's. They stared at each other for a time before Donier lay back on the ground to try to sleep. It would be evening soon enough, and they would be on the march again.

•••

The Shadows did not come for water the next morning, or later at midday. Masiph sat waving at the buzzing gnats and flies which had descended upon him with the heat of the afternoon. His half-closed eyes peered over at Nustef. He had tried to clean the second's wound earlier in the morning with the last of his water, but had given up struggling with the stiff body, fearing that he would do more harm than good. The smell was enough to turn his stomach for the rest of the morning, and he satisfied himself with wrapping the wound with the last of the rags he had made from his outer robe.

Something had happened, but what? He repeated the thought

aloud. They had not come three times now. Nothing stood to reason. He cursed the missed opportunities their absence presented that he had failed to summon the will to take advantage of. It was what, two days now that he had been unwilling to stir from this room? Perhaps more. It was so hard to tell anymore. The days and nights bled together, an unending sort of nightmare that he could not dislodge himself from. The far corner was filled with his piss and shit and the remains of the fruit he had eaten, all of which only made the flies and stench worse.

His dreams were of the devourer, arising now and soon to be loose upon this realm, when he managed to escape to sleep. He had another as he lay back and let the heat and stench of the room wash over him, and he was able to surrender to that sensation of humming numbness, dissipating for the time being his fear.

He awoke near evening and could tell by the shadows in the room that the sun was far in its descent. It was already past the time when the Shadow Men normally came, and there was no sound of them below. If they had come already he would have awoken sooner—in fact, he had drifted in and out of consciousness the whole afternoon, as though under a fever. He listened awhile longer as birds sang back and forth below.

He sat up, looking around, and saw what was there. There was a moment where his thoughts were like clouds drifting clear to reveal the empty sky in all its rapturous blue, and he shuddered. He gathered up his shield and spear and sword and made his way to the garden and the well below. He drank his fill and replenished his canteen. Most of the fruit was rotting on the trees, but he took some time with the light that remained and gathered as much as was salvageable, putting some in the pockets of his inner robe and the rest in his shield. Then he went out into the streets.

They were silent, an empty calm permeating the dusk. It felt like a place formerly inhabited, now abandoned to whatever wild creatures might find their way through its avenues from the desert. He breathed deeply and looked around at the various crumbling edifices that surrounded him, and started down the street going south, back the way he had come.

•••

Blood and liquid quicksilver drenched everything as he

struggled to regain consciousness. It felt strange on his skin, as though it might shift states even now. In another time, another place, he might have marveled at the sensation. His mouth felt raw and he could taste blood. When he tried to sit up, the full weight of what he had just endured settled on him again. There was nothing that did not hurt. Every miniscule element of his body seemed wrecked beyond repair.

He tried to remember, squinting at the ruins and bodies around him. There was glass in everything, and his own skin was cut and burned. He could see against the wall where scaffolding had been set, though it was difficult to tell now what all had been there. The bodies of the dead all looked unfamiliar, creatures from another realm. He did not recognize them. Something had been destroyed, and he had been a part of it, that much he knew.

His name was Vyissan, but that meant little to him. There were others, but he couldn't quite recall them, names or faces. In time, perhaps, though he did not know where they were—or where he was, for that matter. Every thought was a struggle, as if the tendons connecting him were missing or had been torn apart and haphazardly strung together. The pieces were wrong.

He coughed and felt the remnants of flame in his chest. It was all throughout the air too, a heavy, disgusting smell. Maybe it had all come from him. He was a dragon who had spent all his flames down to the last ember and now was left with a cold and empty belly. A husk of a thing.

He crawled out of the room, wanting to escape, to get aboveground. How had he come to be here, so far from the sun? It was a painstaking effort, and he nearly wept when he came to the stairs, but he managed them too. He was dizzy with the effort when he finally reached the top. But he kept going, not daring to stop, because he did not know if he could begin again if he did.

Finally, though, he did halt, the pain too much for him to continue, and then he did weep. Every breath left him swimming in agony. He stayed there, somewhere in the darkness, the smell of earth all around him, and in the distance the stench of flame.

30

Phariayh waited for darkness to return before she dared to leave her hiding place. She was lightheaded from lack of food, and her throat ached from thirst when she emerged, but her gaze was steady and her heart still beat, which she counted as a triumph after her escape from the mob the night before. The camp and the desert lay behind her and, after a moment's hesitation, she turned her back on them and headed deeper into the city. There was nothing there for her anymore but to scavenge and pray to her ancestors that they might spare her. But she had no ancestors, and there was no future there.

She did not know what to expect to find in the ruins of the city. Food and water, hopefully. The Shadows were here as well, though. Part of her wanted to find them, to see them for herself, and part of her was terrified of what might happen to her if she did.

She did not have long to wait, for as she wandered north and east up the city streets, she came upon a half-dozen Shadow Men in an open courtyard of a hollowed-out building hurriedly gathering their belongings and putting them into packs. One man kept watch as they worked, but he was facing to the west and did not see Phariayh as she crept forward. It seemed clear that this had been their camp while they had battled in the city and now they were preparing to withdraw. Were all the Shadows fleeing, she wondered? If so, her time would be short.

After crouching within the deeper shadows of another building, her thoughts warring in her head, Phariayh stepped out into the street and approached the men, making no effort to disguise her steps. She was nearly at the collapsed wall that circled the courtyard when one of the Shadows noticed her and hissed at his fellows. The one on guard whirled around and leveled his sword at her, saying something in a commanding tone. Phariayh stopped and raised her hands, trying to keep the fear from her face, though of course they would not be able to see that.

The guard approached, looking her over for weapons, and gestured for one of his companions to watch her while he went up the road to see if there was anyone else with her. When he was satisfied that she was alone, he returned and said something to her. A question, she judged, by his tone.

"I have been abandoned," Phariayh said in reply, hoping that perhaps they might understand a little of the Renian tongue. She was met with a blank face, and the man repeated his question. "I'm hungry," she said, trying a different tact, miming eating with her hands.

The guard nodded and gestured to one of the Shadows crouched over the packs, who brought forward a bit of bread, which he offered to Phariayh. She took it eagerly and tore at the it with her teeth. The bread was soft and tasted of a grain she did not know. As she ate, the guard said something to the other Shadows and pointed at her. The others nodded, and she looked from shadowed face to shadowed face as she chewed, trying to discern what they were talking about.

When she was finished, the guard handed her his canteen and she poured it back without heed, almost emptying it. The guard laughed and said something, which caused the others to chuckle. He gestured to the man with the bread, and he offered her another piece. This she ate slowly, savoring it, offering an invocation to her ancestors for this kindness while trying not to think of what might follow it.

Once she had finished, the guard uttered what was unmistakably an order and the other Shadows slung their packs over their shoulders and set off down the street. The guard turned to her and gestured for her to follow them, his eyes unreadable in the darkness. Phariayh did, and he fell in step behind her, and they walked through the night out of the city and into the desert until the sun began to stain the horizon.

•••

Donier's shoulders ached where the poles of the carriage were set, and a lancing pain stabbed up his back with nearly every step, but he forced himself to ignore it as best he could. If he fell, which was what he feared most, he did not know what the Shadows would do to him, but he assumed the worst. So he kept on, step after step, each one an unbearable agony. Death might be preferable to this, but still his soul would not allow him to surrendur and embark on that terrible journey to Ulternon's Hall.

As with the day before, they began to march shortly before nightfall, after the Shadows had come around to give them their daily sustenance. This time there was more bread with fruits and nuts baked into it. After so many days with little or no food, it had been a feast, though he knew it would not sustain him long.

The sky was cloudless, as it always seemed to be here in the desert, and the moon was just past full, so they went forward through the hills and rock without difficulty. The Shadows were silent for the most part as they walked, and they moved with an ease that spoke of a deep familiarity, both with the path they were on and the night itself. The surrounding desert was quiet too, their unanswered footsteps marking the solitude of their passage.

They were allowed to rest for half an hour sometime after midnight, the moon's descent begun. Most of his fellow prisoners collapsed to the ground and slept, but Donier was unable to, for in spite of how exhausted and sore his body was, he felt strangely alert. The Shadow Men huddled in groups nearby eating a meal, none of them speaking. He watched them through the darkness without emotion, without even thought, aware only of the immense silence that surrounded them, no wind stirring. A still place.

The movement, when it came, startled him. He heard nothing of their approach until they were nearly through the encampment. Dozens and dozens of the Shadows passed by, in loose formation, not acknowledging their fellows, who in turn barely glanced from their meals. They were moving quickly, and were gone from sight and hearing almost before Donier even realized they were there at all. Not long after, they began the march again.

The rest of the night passed with the deadening clank of the irons and step after step, each more impossible than the last, and each somehow followed by another. After a time the rest of the realm vanished and there was only the weight of the carriage and his own slowing steps. It was no longer a matter of whether or not he could continue; his legs seemed to move of their own accord, his whole body apart from itself.

It was nearing morning, the light creeping into the sky at the edge of the eastern horizon, when they stopped again, but the Shadow Men made no gesture for them to place their load down. In fact, they paid their prisoners no mind at all, looking at something nearby on the ground. It took Donier a moment to discern that there were bodies there—two, from what he could see. They were Shadows, and a change in the air told him they had been there for some time. From his vantage point he could see that the tolotes had already been at the bodies, marring them beyond recognition.

Three of the Shadows went over to the bodies, standing over them in a contemplative pose. Donier expected that the prisoners would soon be asked to bury or burn these Shadows, but that was not the case. No one stirred, though the atmosphere was one of invocation, or so it seemed so to him. At last the three began to move. It took Donier a moment to recognize what they were doing, and when he did he was sickened with horror.

They were dancing, slowly at first, and then faster until they were an unspeakable frenzy of limbs and ecstasy. The others watched solemnly, until at some unspoken signal the dancers stopped and returned to the ranks and they began to march again. By morning's light they were beyond the hills in a long valley, ascending to a wide plain that continued unbroken as far as the eye could see.

GLOSSARY OF TERMS

Abapolly: mythical demon from Kragi

Ad Eselte: title of emperor in Renuih

Adept: practioner of alkemya

Aesen: canal in Darrhyn

Alkemy: the latent power within all elements that can be released by transmutation

Alkemya: the practice and study

Anchonites: monastic priest in Renuih

Ardeh: animal, raised for its wool, milk and meat

Asieren: Ad Ezern paradise in Renuih

Aslyn: leaf that is chewed

Astral: aspect of elements that contains alkemy

Asyl: psychotropic nectar

Ceinobyte: Renian priest

Celes: Ad Reteln paradise in Renuih

Cohort: Craitolian amy unit

Corenedor: Renian officer in the army or Watch

Craitol: Realm of, as well as capital of the Realm; westernmost realm in all the lands

Cureders: Craitolian priest

Dala: beans, drink brewed from

Darrhyn: imperial city of Renuih

Devew: city and river in Kragi

Disciple: practitioner of alkemya, Adept's subordinate

Dravasyl: drinkery in Darrhyn

Elen: city in Renuih

Enir: a distinct religious sect of the Renian people

Enir Republics: once part of Renuih; now independent city states along the coast between Renuih and Craitol, south of the desert; inhabited by those of the Enir sect

Eresnan: River between Darrhyn and Sylaron in Renuih

Esyln: jewel of the Renian Empire in the desert; now a ruins inhabited by the Shadow Men

Fegh: city in Kragi Province

Gver: Craitolian lord, governor of a particular territory

Haigah: mountain city on the border between Kragi and Craitol; a mountain pass

The Hashil: central boulevard in Lastl

Hasierren: Lasisen sanctuary in Craitol

Hessen: Enir Republic

Hesite: district in Takyl

Hezier: ruler in the Enir Republics

Hueithel: neighborhood in Darrhyn

Hjai: second to a Vazeir in Renian Imperial administration.

Isinan: a street in Darrhyn

Jetthir: leader of a quadra, officer in the Renian army or Watch. Lower in rank than a Corenedor.

Kastril: Renian fruit

Kenir: coin of Renuih

Kragi: province in the north of Craitol; once an independent realm

Kulez: northern city in Renuih

Kylep: city in Craitol; seat of a Gver Byuvir

Lasisen: a sect of worshipers of Senteur in Craitol

Lastl: city in Craitol; seat of a Gver Keleprai

Lethle: city in Kragi Province

Luessan: one of the three eastern kingdoms that broke away from the Renuih Empire

Luisel: town in Renuih

Magister: officer of law in Craitol

Magisterium: building of the Magistery

Magistery: officers, or the office itself

Melinon: Craitolian goddess of the earth

Mgetir: island south of Craitol

Morning, Midday, Evening: factions in Craitol

Mythres: powder made from flowers native to Kragi

Nrai: port city in Craitol; one of the contestants in the Sea Challenge; seat of Gver Assuard

Nohritai: nobility in Renuih

Nuerrallah: one of the great sages of Reniuh

Qraul: ruler of Craitol

Quadra: unit of the armed forces in Renuih

Quicksilver: an element capable of inhabiting all constitutions simultaneously and decaying the astral of any substance

Pyrsedies: forts guarding the desert frontier in Craitol

Psyel: city in Craitol; seat of Gver Pervelte

Rakai: port city in Craitol; involved in Sea Challenge

Renuih: Empire in the east, former rulers of the desert

Sanader: religious authority in Craitol; usually has authority over a particular city or region

Senteur: Craitolian god of the heavens

Shadow Men: the people of the desert; also referred to as Shadows or by other pejoratives (demons, beasts, etc.)

Suliher: honorific for those in the Renian Watch or Army

Sylaron: major port city in Renuih

Takyl: city in Craitol; seat of Gver Duirhe

Tolote: coyote-like animal of the desert

Tson: city in Craitol; seat of Gver Hythel

Tuissar: Enir Republic

Uenam: district in Darrhyn

Ulternon: Craitolian god of the dead

Usgelt: city in Kragi Province

Vazeir: imperial administrator in Renuih

Watch: protectors of the imperial city Darrhyn

Xln: port city in Craitol, involved in Sea Challenge

Yuehilth: prison in Darrhyn

Yseltez: city in Craitol; seat of Gver Issilar

ABOUT THE AUTHOR

Clint Westgard is the author of The Shadow Men Trilogy and the science fiction epic The Sojourner Cycle, the first volume of which, The Forgotten, was published in 2015. In addition, he has published a work of historical fantasy set in colonial Peru, *The Maleficio Chronicles*, and a retelling of the Minotaur legend, *The Trials of the Minotaur*. Clint Westgard lives in Calgary, Alberta.

ALSO BY CLINT WESTGARD

The Forgotten

Volume One of The Sojourners Cycle

Who is David Aeida? And what does he know that has so many
people pursuing him?

David doesn't know. He can't remember anything about who he is.
But he finds himself ensnared in a vicious conflict between a
religious cult and a guild that patrols the crossings between
multiple universes. They will both stop at nothing to gain whatever
knowledge he possesses. Most dangerous of all, is the implacable
hunter, known only as the Seeker, who has his own reasons for
wanting to find David.

His only hope is to recover his memories before they do. His only
ally is a woman named Meredith, and she definitely knows more
than she is telling...

Spanning both universes and the human mind, *The Forgotten* is an
unforgettable science fiction thriller that questions the very nature
of identity. It is the first volume of the *Sojourners Cycle*, an epic that
will encompass the fates of universes and humanity itself.

ALSO BY CLINT WESTGARD

The Apostate

Volume Two of The Sojourners Cycle

Laila has only one goal in mind. To have her revenge upon the Grand Regent for all he has done to her. First, though, she needs to find her way across the universes.

That is easier said than done. The Grand Regent's agents are still pursuing her. As is the Society of Travellers. And the Seeker lurks somewhere, waiting for his moment to strike.

Laila has a plan, though, and a few tricks of her own. But she will discover that not everything is at seems. For the war she has given her life to hides a far greater conflict.

Spanning multiple universes and the complexities of the human mind, *The Apostate*, continues the incredible journey begun in The Forgotten. The second volume of *The Sojourners Cycle* is an unforgettable science fiction epic that encompasses the fates of universes and humanity itself.

ALSO BY CLINT WESTGARD

The Maleficio Chronicles

Luisa is always more than she appears. Rumor and mystery surround her. And strange events seem to follow wherever she goes.

Born in Lima, City of Kings, to a noble family, her father so fears her true nature that he banishes her to a convent. There she falls under the suspicion of the Inquisition and decides to flee.

Disguised as a man, she embarks upon a series of wild adventures, dueling, carousing, and gambling her way across colonial Peru. But everything changes when someone recognizes her for what she truly is, and soon she finds herself fighting for her very survival.

In a world where she will always stand apart, Luisa undergoes a strange journey, marked by betrayal and murder, terrible powers and mysterious strangers. *The Maleficio Chronicles* is her incredible confession and a story like no other.

ALSO BY CLINT WESTGARD

The Trials of the Minotaur

In the fifth year of the rule of Auten the One Eyed a minotaur is born to one of Colosi's most important families.

Taken from his mother as a newborn, exiled and cast from his family, the minotaur vows to return to the imperial city and take his rightful place as a patrician in the empire. But the patriarch of the family, his grandfather, will stop at nothing to see this blemish to his honor destroyed.

And so begins an epic journey, through lands beyond imagining, marked by despair and exile, triumph and betrayal. At its heart lies a quest to be free.